SIREN

THE CRASHED SERIES BOOK TWO

INTERNATIONAL BEST SELLER

KERRI ANN

Copyright

Siren is a work of fiction. All names, characters, locations, and incidents are the products of the author's imagination or are used fictitiously. Any resemblance to actual events, locales, or persons, living or dead, is entirely coincidental.

Formatting & Cover Design by KP Designs

Wyatt Crown was mine. I was his.

I'd been cherished by a man that had once cherished nothing. Feeling his hands on my body. His breath on my skin. The soft whisper of him caresses my soul. He was imprinted on my soul. In that moment I didn't feel alone anymore. I do now.

After the crash, I fear the outcome of those I love. I'm afraid as my world crumbles. Calling out in the cold darkness, the lack of a reply crushes me. My heart breaks. Shredding into a million pieces, it leaves me broken and scarred.

Why am I going through this again?

Chapter One

The heart knows what it wants. The soul cries out for its mate, and loss is inevitable. There's no way around death. Death sucks.

I watch the rose petals fall all around me like heavy snowflakes crashing to the ground. They're warped, tangled, and coated in dark blood—a color that consumes you in darkness and despair. Something has happened—something epic and life-changing.

Will I survive it?

Do I want to? Has anyone else lived? Am I dead, watching from afar the carnage of the Reaper and his evil will? I've been a party to so much death, you'd think I could handle the outcome. The crushing pall of disaster as it leeches into the pavement taints my already broken soul.

There were three of us in the car, three of us alive. Three people who had finally had a moment where we all felt content. Our appetite for mental mayhem had come to a boiling point, and I was finally able to feel at peace for a few brief moments.

Am I hopeful that we're all alive? That no one perished? Yes. For that I would be eternally grateful.

If we're to live another day, I will do everything I can to correct my shortcomings, the family's pain, and that of our lives moving forward.

I'll find a way to fix it all.

Feeling tired and exhausted, I drift off. Dreaming, I'm hoping for a change in my future—in *our* futures.

Chapter Two

Wyatt

A

fter the dust settles, and the last vestiges of beauty still hang in the air, that's when you have the best memories of your current dream. The flashes. The whispers of greatness.

Stretched out on my monster Cali King, with thick fluffy pillows, lying comfortably in my home, I wake to her beside me, with her strawberry-colored hair fanning out around her, she's enticing and erotic. Her prone, naked, glorious body is strapped to the bed, spread out like a buffet. *My Circe.*

Searching, exploring, and teasing every inch of her body has been what's kept me off the track today. She knows how to pull every stop, where to nip, full-on bite, and crush every expectation I've ever had. I've never had inhibitions that seemed untouchable. They're unnecessary, and easily overcome.

She's pushed them further.

This is what I want my reality to be. *This* is a moment I've always hoped for. Clarity in my own mind.

Watching the vision fall out of focus, a tightness shoots through every nerve in my body.

"Clear!"

The dream scatters like smoke. My clarity is removed, disappointing me as it dissipates. As the sounds of home dissolve, other sounds become heightened. Motions become exponentially crisp. The sound of blood rushing through my ears almost drowns it out.

With a sharp pain radiating through my body, the loud beeping of machines and shouting voices increases.

"I got him back," someone says. The words are clouded, but the urgency in their tone is unmistakable. "Get him in. Let's go." The words are rushed and authoritative.

Opening my eyes, my lashes wipe away the whispering ghosts that clouded my sight. Blinking past them, looking around as best I can, a face I don't recognize comes into view. Her russet hair is pulled into a tight ponytail. Her face is makeup free, and her bright green eyes remind me of Circe. She's pretty, but she's not her.

What happened to us? My thoughts feel important, but they slip away quickly.

Everything is hazy, and my memory fades into a dense fog. "Where are they?" I ask, my voice gravelly.

"Sorry?" Bending low, the woman pulls the mask gently away from my mouth. "Repeat that, please?"

Like the words will be clearer the second time. Every word is a fight. Trying my best anyway, I force them out. "Where. Are. They?"

"We'll get you out of here soon. Let's look after you. You're our priority, Mr. Crown." Her voice is like listening to music underwater. With a look of sadness, she produces a counterfeit smile before pulling a blanket across my chest, flitting with the edges. "You can find out about them after, okay?"

Why does she seem worried? What happened? And where the fuck am I?

Taking the woman's horrible advice, I force myself to relax. I try to remember where we were, what we were doing, and I'm finding it hard to think coherently as everything is broken and splintered. Time is not my friend.

That *dream.* Was it real? It felt tangible. If I can't remember what happened, then I want *that* back. In this condition, though, I can't argue with her. I have no energy. My body is tired, and I can't even lift my head. My body feels like it's being held down by weights.

Fuck, I *feel* like I've raced for hours.

Resigning against the numbing pain, I slump back to accept her ministrations.

Looking around us, it seems we're on a freeway. The lights are dim, the sun is gone, and the moon is just cresting the sky. Nothing is discernible. Feeling the gurney jolt as we ride across the pavement, it lifts as we enter the back of the open ambulance with a thunk. The lights inside are painfully bright against the stark white interior of the cabin, making me squint.

"We're going to be moving shortly, sir." Moving my head to look for the voice, I see a muscular guy, who's about my age, pulling out tubes, wires, and plugs and such. "I have to get an IV set, and you'll hear some beeping from the monitors. Can you concentrate on that?"

I hear his desperate urgency to keep me awake, but it's hard to focus.

"Squeeze my hand if you understand."

Placing as much pressure as I can into my grip, he squeezes mine. The big guy smiles, then continues on with what he was doing. Pulling in shallow breaths, one after the other, I try to concentrate on his actions.

"Tasha, we're good to go."

As the ambulance moves, the male attendant shuffles around the cabinets, pulling out this and that, flicking switches, pulling cords, and adjusting the blankets that are lying across my body.

Lying still, I feel out my injuries. The cataloguing keeps me present in the here and now. First is toes. Left foot works. Right foot's good. Next, I try my hands. Right's working. Left...nothing. I try again, but still nothing.

"My. Hand?" Croaking out the words.

"It's in a splint. You broke your forearm and wrist when you crashed."

Crashed?

I *crashed*? I never crash. On the track, my life is a series of crashes, busted bones, split lips, fractured hips and swollen fingers. But on the freeway, on side streets, and in a fucking family car, *I don't crash*.

"What. Happened?" I ask slowly. I'm hoping he'll be the one who gives me the answers I need.

"You were sideswiped by a transport on the Intercoastal. They extricated you."

"Where. Are. They?" Forcing enough air into my lungs to speak in a single breath, he pulls the blanket higher, resting it right below my chin. Again, I see the same crestfallen look on his face that I saw on the woman.

"They'll be coming along. You were the last one out. The car was squashed up so tight against the rail, it took them a bit to get to you."

"Are. They. Safe?"

Reaching across to push a few buttons on the monitor, he looks me in the eyes. I don't like what I'm seeing. "I can't say right now, Mr. Crown. We'll just have to wait and see." Filling a syringe, he reaches down and says, "This should help you with the pain."

Immediately, I feel a cool rush travel through my arm. My eyes grow heavy and my mind calms. Whatever was in that syringe has now made me pliant and serene. It's not the first time, and it certainly won't be the last time for me either.

****

As they check monitors, lines, fluid levels, and various listings on the chart, the people scrambling around the room continue on without speaking to me directly. I hear them ask someone how I am, how my pain is being managed, and if I need more or less drugs to deal with the pain, but not once do they ask *me*. Recognizing the voice that's answering, I know it's my sister Doll. Why aren't they asking me?

How *are* the others? Where's Circe? Where's Mother?

Everything is so confusing. Everything is out of place. I remember fire trucks, ambulances, race cars, bikes in the mountain, family fights, and *her*.

Always her. Her brilliant green eyes and her radiant red hair. Her sarcasm, strong wit, and fire. All I want to know is how she is? How *they* are.

Fuck me. I'm tired in all the ways that count. Wanting to rest my eyes, that's when the loud beeping starts its incessant squealing again. Alarms sound on the monitors and nurses run in, cussing like truckers, and immediately I feel cold.

That's when *they* appear. I see them. The specters are standing by in the shadows, awaiting me and mine. I don't wish to give them the joy of gathering another Crown into their midst, so I fight.

I'll fight because I have to.

Chapter Three

Circe

Shattered, marbled, star-faced glass surrounds me. As each one lays around me in a thousand improper pieces, they wait to be pieced back together. It's like the most treacherous, and trickiest jigsaw puzzle imaginable. I feel broken. I remember when everything was solid, when my life felt contained, and held promise.

"Miss? Can you hear me?" I feel as if I'm drowning in a pool of mud. It's thick and gooey. It won't allow me to budge. My tongue is thick, my mind is hazy, and all of it leaves me unable to form a coherent answer. Even though I feel the motions of others tugging, pulling, and shoving me as they scurry to free us from our bonds, I feel far away and disconnected.

"She's in and out of consciousness," someone says.

"Where's that stretcher?" Another yells franticly into the deafness of the night.

This shouldn't be happening to *me.*

This can't be happening again.

Life isn't that cruel to do this to me twice, is it? The end result will be just as catastrophic as it was before, and I'm scared by that.

Once, there was this shattering effect on my life, and at that time, I had the courage to set myself on the only path available. I picked my ass up, without bitching about what shouldn't have happened, and I learned how to pass grief by. It was like watching headlights in the rearview mirror as a car slips into the night. This time, though, I don't think I can keep it together.

"Miss, I'm going to help you out of there." A kind and gentle voice breaks through the murkiness. Engaging my attention for a split second, they say, "I need you to stay awake for me."

Awake? It's too hard. Staying awake seems impossible. I want to sleep. I want to let it all fall to the Fates. I want to free myself of the repetitive pain that I know awaits me. There'd be no more cares about who I make happy, who I've disappointed, and no more worries about...well, just no more worries.

After promising myself I'd never be here again, I struggle with the end result. Feeling weak and unable to deal with the pain, I'm crushed that I may have no choice.

Muffled voices speak in somber tones, conversing around me. Vaguely, I make out snippets of, "Is she," or "Is he?" And even though they're just small questions that are denuded of inflection, they convey an awful weight. They must be accustomed to this carnage, this *Death*. Boy, did I notice *him*. Feeling the exact moment when Death crept across my soul, he was close. Close enough that laying out my hand, I'd feel him brush up against my skin. His decrepit grin was disturbing, and that sickly smile passed his features as he took someone from my life. Even though I had no idea who he'd taken, I still felt his cool lips touch my cheek.

Death had kissed me on the way by.

My body doesn't react to the cool of the night, even as it kisses my bare and bleeding skin. I don't feel the warmth of helping hands touching me as they work to free me from the tangled mess either. Disengaging myself, it's like I'm a spectator in the peripheral, where everything is detached and disconnected.

As time passes in a blink, or what feels like a blink, I drift away.

I'm wishing to vanish.

****

Awaking to the rushing of doctors, nurses, various assistants and interns, it was strangely unsettling. My mind compartmentalized them into the background. They're there, but in their own dark world. Bouncing and popping into my clouded sight, they dissipate like an unsettled dream. When opening my eyes after a restless sleep, this feels just the same. It's disconnected, discombobulated, and rough.

Beside my head is a woman in deep pink scrubs leaning over me. She's so close, I feel her breath on my face.

"Jackson, I need you on this side."

The lovely lady pulls at my eyelids, flashing a light, and gently checks my head with her fingers. Pushing and poking, it feels like lightning striking my brain. Every nerve in my head screams. The tang of copper coats my tongue, and my lips feel like they're coated in flour. My nose is scratchy, and I so badly want to ask for a Kleenex. I'm afraid, though, that my brains will spill out.

"Miss Maco? I'm Callie Ethan, your surgeon. You can call me Dr. Callie. You have a mighty large contusion on your forehead, a broken wrist, and three broken ribs. Two of them are sticking out of your shirt, love. I believe you have extensive internal bleeding." Tugging lightly on a few cables being suctioned to my chest before talking again, she smiles down at me. "Is there anything you can tell me that will help to better assess you?"

Opening my mouth to speak, my head screams to halt all motions. Got it, body. Point taken. No speaking.

"Do you have any allergies, or anything we should know about, honey? Blink twice if you do." When she says 'honey' comes out smooth, with a southern drawl, like 'hawnnie.'

I blink once.

"Okay, Circe. Can I call you Circe?" She smiles, knowing that I won't answer her question. "We'll be taking you to surgery in a few minutes. Don't you worry none, sweetie. You're in good hands." Her soft smile makes me feel comfortable, even though my instincts scream to run like hell.

"You'll wake feeling refreshed, and happier than a bug in June."

Seeing her inject a liquid into the IV that rests in my hand, I feel a cool rush.

In less than to the count of three, I'm out.

****

Beep, beep. Beep, beep. Beep, beep.

Coming to, the machines constant chatter in the background is a soft, consistent hum. It's almost melodic. I slowly open my scratchy eyes and take in the space. There's a set of stark white curtains, a clock on the wall that says three-fifteen, and other than my prone body, there's not much else. Everything aches, though, so I bet that's a good sign.

As the door to the room opens, allowing the sounds from the outside in, I joyously anticipate the visitor I want to see. I only need to know that they're alive. As my heart rate increases with giddy joy, the curtains are thrown open wide. In her bright outfit, the lovely southern surgeon walks in. Leaning over the edge of my bed and smiles.

"Well, sugar. Glad you're back."

Holding the petite flashlight in her hand, she sweeps it back and forth across my eyes, then flicks her fingers. She's smiling and humming to her own musical tune as she removes her stethoscope from around her shoulders and begins to count beats. When she's done, she asks, "How you feelin?" as she absently goes over my damages.

I run my tongue along my teeth. My mouth still feels like it's stuck with road tar. My eyes are weighty, and I feel like there are small cars attached to each lid.

As I say nothing, she continues to speak, as if I gave her the answer she required. "I won't keep you. We'll be moving you from here to a new room in a bit. And don't worry none, Circe. We'll take good care of you."

Checking the readings on the incessant beeping machine, she pushes a few buttons to silence it. Turning back to me, she pulls the blanket back to look at my chest, lifting the bandages. "We fixed up your ribs, your wrist, the punctured lung, and the hole in your spleen. Plus, I sutured that nasty gouge on your head. After a little plastic surgery, you should be scar free."

Now I understand why it's so difficult to breathe; I have a punctured lung. Great.

Flicking a few switches, checking the wrappings on my incisions, Dr. Callie tucks the blanket up tight again.

"I'll check on you again in a bit, darlin', so get some rest." Smiling, she wanders away, leaving me curious. Where are the others? I want to ask. I want to know. But my body is sore, my mind is clouded, and my soul is exhausted.

As I'm dragged back to lala-land almost immediately, I find myself closing my eyes and forgetting what's so important. Memories blur, bringing pieces together haphazardly, reminding me of how fate decides our path without our intervention. I drift off, unable to stop it.

My life was going in a better direction, right?

Or was this just an intermission dragging me toward the evil plot maker's finale?

Chapter Four

Wyatt

BEEP, BEEP, BEEP.

That goddamn monitor sings, signaling I'm still alive. Thank fuck.

My body doesn't move, even as my mind screams at me to get up. I've been worse than this. I need to stop being such a pussy. *Shove some dirt in it and get up, Crown*, it says, but nothing happens. I'm trapped.

Fucking perfect. Goddamn awesome. I can't even fathom the words to express how *fucking amazing* this is. This sucks big hairy man nuts.

It *feels* like I'm awake, but I know I'm not.

Noticing the nurse, I watch as she flicks buttons on the monitor, switching lines on my arm, pulling bags hanging overhead, and neatly tucking me back into the blanket tightly. I feel like an infant. I wonder if this is how it is when we're babies? Feeling everything, hearing all of it, but unable to react. I want to speak out. I want to fucking yell at the top of my lungs. But nothing happens.

Do we understand it, but have no control? Seeing the world, unable to express motion and fear; if it's like that, it must be daunting. For me, I know it is.

Passing in front of my sight like an apparition, I attempt to yell out my frustration at the nurse. Nothing audibly happens.

Fuck, that makes me laugh. To her, I'm just a body on the bed. I'm nobody of importance in her everyday life.

Go figure. My nickname comes to fruition. I'm *Casper the Fucking Ghost*.

How many more shitstick problems can I endure? You'd think I'd had enough in my lifetime. I guess not.

The worst part about all of this; I don't know about the others.

How are they?

Are they alive?

I can't even ask.

Chapter Five

Circe

D

ays later, I've spent more hours asleep than awake.

"Circe. How are we feeling, darlin'?" Dr. Callie's musical accent is adorable. The way she says 'darlin' comes out without an r.

"I feel like an army convoy of Humvee's ran me down, with road spikes imbedded in the tires." Pushing a breath out, my voice is scratchy, and it aches to talk. I guess it will be that way for a while. I've never punctured a lung before.

Letting a carefree laugh escape, Dr. Callie pulls the blanket back, inspecting my hand. The cast is itchy as fuck, but I know it's for the best. Even if I wanted to, I'd avoid smashing it to pieces, or running it under water, mainly because I'm afraid of the sweet Southern Belle. My feeling is that there's more to her than the sweet and adorable lady she portrays.

"Well, love. Don't think you'll be runnin' out of here anytime soon. I'll place bets it'll be a while before we send you packin'. You still have to deal with a therapist and physio. You don't leave until you can walk on your own power."

"What? No." How the hell am I gonna pay for that? Sure, my job pays for a bit, but what about the rest? I'm as poor as you can get. "I can't afford. Staying here. Dr. Callie." Being conked out, I didn't think about the costs. I thought about him and sleeping as they drugged me over and over. The last time I had an accident of this magnitude, I had a trust fund family. Using all my savings to move back to the States, I have nothing to pay for a hospital stay like this.

Dr. Callie turns, grinning, tucking the blanket back around my arm. "No worries at all. Your stay has been cared for. Just concentrate on getting better."

"How? Who?" I sound like I'm squeaking.

"Your bills are cared for. I can't tell you who, but it's not somethin' you need to worry about. Get rest, doctor's orders. Your body won't repair without sleep."

Great, *more* sleep, *more* bed rest, *more* physiotherapists. *More* learning to grip, pull, and hold. *More* learning my body all over again. This time, though, I'll be indebted to someone.

Fantastic. It wasn't my intention to repeat my past failures. Seems *my* Fates are a sneaky set of bitches.

Checking my monitors, adjusting some of the levels, Dr. Callie goes over my chart like she has every few hours today. Smiling that wide grin, showcasing her perfect teeth, Dr. Callie turns, about to leave me once more.

As she's about to close the curtains back up, I ask, "Doc. How—" She cuts me off. "I can't say, Circe. I'm sorry."

"But. Who's. Paying. My bills?" I know NASCAR will fit some of it, but who's helping beyond that? Feeling out of breath, I pause, giving the doctor the time she needs to interject.

"I can't tell you." Stopping my line of questioning with harshly spoken words, I feel myself fall a little inside.

Pulling in a tight breath, I rush the words quickly past my tongue. "Can you. Tell me about them. At least?"

Stopping before exiting the room, realizing her brashness, she spins around to answer me with an apologetic look. "I'm so sorry, Circe. I can't tell you. Really, I wish I could. I can't give you confidential patient information. You're not related. You weren't listed as family, and even though you were in the car with them, I can't tell you their progress. I'm sorry." Nodding my understanding, even though I'm on the verge of pouring my eyes out, the doctor pulls the door shut behind her.

Feeling cut off from everything and everyone, I'm overwhelmed. Being left alone to my despair, I curl up as comfortably as I can on my wooden pallet. Tears stream down my face in heavy rivulets, even as the sobbing hurts my chest. It's painful, but nothing compared to the loss my heart is enduring.

Pulling the light cotton blankets close, drifting off to sleep, my body and mind are both utterly and hopelessly exhausted. How much more can I be expected to take in one lifetime? How much pain, suffering, solitude and loss can one soul endure?

I can't do this alone.

Wyatt, where are you?

Chapter Six

Wyatt

China, I'm going to give you the straight goods." The doctor, a petite lady, no more than five foot five, maybe five-six at most, has pulled up a chair to sit across from my sister.

Watching as Doll talks to her, I'm horribly sorry that she's in this spot. She's dealing with it so well, sure, but it's not her place. Keeping a brave face and looking the part of a matriarch—like mother trained her to be—she's stoic, poised, and harnessing her inner Marca Crown. Nothing would make mother prouder.

"Your brother was in a bad way, and there's no way to sugar coat it. He's broken and beat. We've placed him in a medical coma for now."

Nodding mechanically, Doll accepts the information she's being given. "How long will he need that?"

"It's hard to say, really." Flicking her teeth with her tongue, the doctor grimaces. "I won't lie. I think it's going to be a long recovery. Everything is going to be touch and go for a bit. There was a lot of damage to his body, and the swelling on his brain will take time to come down."

Seeing the strain and stress of it landing in Doll's lap sucks. I'm the big brother. I'm the one that's supposed to take up the slack, giving her a boost in a crisis, not the other way around. "Well, I guess I should get things brought in. Is it okay that I stay here?"

"Of course, sweets." She hands Doll some paperwork. "We'll be your only contact. No other team will bother you. If there's anything you need from me or the staff, just ask."

Taking the thin sheets, she lays them on the bed, across my still body. "I'll ask Jamieson, my other brother, to grab me some things from the house."

Rising, she pats Doll on the shoulder. "As I said, if you need anything, don't hesitate to ask, Mrs. Crown."

Her slip of the formal greeting isn't missed. Vehemently shaking her head, Doll informs her, "I'm Miss. Not Mrs. Crown."

"Of course. I'll leave you to your family then."

"Thank you, Dr. Callie."

Closing the door behind her, my sister slinks down into the chair. She relaxes now that the doctor has left, her tired body taking in deep, calming breaths. I see it all crushing her.

Pushing down her pain, Doll talks to me like I'll answer. "Wyatt. There's only so much I can take. You leaving me won't be a part of that. Knowing the outcome of our family, knowing what will happen if you leave me...I *won't* survive this if you leave me alone." Laying her head on the side of the bed, draping an arm across my body, my sister collects her strength. "Tell me I'm selfish. Tell me I'm being a diva. Fuck, tell me anything. Just fight this. I'm going to stay strong, and you're going to live through this. Then you'll get your ass home and show me what it means to be the champion." She taps on my leg, like she's playing the piano. "No faking this just to get Jell-O. No staying in that head of yours any longer than you need to. And for fuck's sake, no darkness! Stay with me, brother."

She's baiting me. Good girl. Push as much as you want. I don't want to be here either. Thinking to myself of what I'd answer her with if given the chance, I talk to her as if she can hear me. "I don't want to be here either, Doll. The longer I'm in this turmoil, I'm not sure I'll come out the same on the other side."

Checking her watch, looking at the numerous texts on her phone, she places it on the pillow beside me. "I'm fucking tired of this." Laying it down, but leaving her hand on me, she says, "Come home, Wyatt."

Chapter Seven

Circe

Day after day, every hour on the hour, a nurse passes through the room, waking me because of my head injury. She then leaves after checking all of my ridiculous monitors, quietly leaving as I ask about *them*. They give me the same answer each time. I hate this.

She won't say, which is worse for my psyche than knowing the horrible truth. Doctor Callie has checked on me daily. She *doesn't* run. She shuts me down each time I ask with a definitive no. That only pisses me off more. I have a feeling they died, but in my bones, it doesn't feel true.

When I'm alert enough, and the cloud of drugs have worn off, I find myself animated and ready to take on anyone. Of course, anytime I become agitated or insistent of answers, they inject me with enough morphine to flatten a pachyderm. They tell me it's "required" for my recovery.

Bullshit, I say. But the worst part of it all is that I can't disagree much. I have this aching feeling that my injuries will hurt like ass once they back off the good drugs. So it's the same, daily. So much so, that I'm almost not inclined to look at the clock and it's passing time.

It's been days, maybe weeks. Heck, it could've been a month to my heart, because all I think about is how this feels so much like before. I'm the one left to deal with the aftermath in my soul.

Shocking myself into my past, my senses can almost taste it. When my sleeping mind drags me back to the past, it's not to happier times. It takes me to times in my life that I've tried to forget quite insistently. Remembering the sights, the smells, and the sounds of the track where Wyatt ruled, I do all I can to think of those happier times with him. Feeling his touch, his soft whispers on my skin, with the dark taunting need of his body and mine together. All of it's a constant reminder that he was becoming mine, and I was his. It pains me not knowing our fate.

Memories can be more damaging than physical pain. When you realize that holding a bad memory at bay is like holding a cloud still, then I wish you good luck with the attempt. I've tried. I have the tears and scars to prove it.

In a haze of mental smoke, everything blends, my family and his—my history and his past. All of those poignant milestones in my life create a jumbled and discombobulated slideshow.

I find myself swimming dangerously in a history that sometimes I had hoped was long forgotten. The feel of the cool ice, the joy of it. It all brings to light harsh reminders of damages to my body and soul. I'm crushed just a touch more by that past and this present.

Chapter Eight

Wyatt

Her back is bowed.

The grip I have on her hair must be nearing a deep throbbing pain, but she moans harder as I pound my cock harshly within. My Siren has captivated me through sex, love, and understanding of my need to slake the ghosts in my mind with thrusts.

The thin bead of sweat that trickles down her backside only drives me deeper, which makes me kick her knees out further. It entices me to hold her that much tighter, and prods me to give her every last drop of my release.

Her folds plump as her orgasm crests, just before sending her over the edge, with me alongside her. I love this, the knowledge that I caused her to be this wanton and desperate for release. Feeling my balls tighten, and my cock swelling to the point of release, I tell her, "You're such a good girl, Siren." Toying with the beads in her ass, pulling them lightly, her muffled sounds increase in pitch. "It's time, love. Don't hold back. Let it take you."

Bending her back further, even with her hands and feet restrained, Circe looks over her shoulder at me. The ball gag stopping her from screaming is neatly in place as she clamps her jaw tight. The look on her face is of pure ecstasy, and is euphoric to me. She takes everything I offer. It's not one-sided either, as that tight cunt of hers owns me. It feels as if a vice is holding me in place, squeezing me, but keeping me tightly within.

I hold out as long as I can, riding her orgasm all the way. The pressure and the tightness—all of it accentuates my pleasure that much more.

She bucks her hips back and forth, as far as the restraints and my knees will allow her. Circe is wild in her insatiable need to extend her enjoyment as long as she can. And I'll let her. I'll give her the room to push the envelope further every time.

Over the past few weeks, during our 'let's try this', the vivacious redhead under me has become bolder. Even something I'd never tried, namely tonight, with tying up our feet together in the bonds has been intriguing. If she moved, I moved. Even where she wanted the clamps placed, I'd have never expected. Placing them on her sensitive folds, the soft sounds of her anticipating each placement as I dragged them across her drenched pussy was tantalizing.

As she slows, my will to hold out crests. After a few long thrusts later in that exquisite heat, I'm come undone. Bending forward, lying across her back, I reach around and remove the clamps from her swollen cunt first. Groaning gently, Circe feels every nerve alight as she comes down, which makes me adore her more.

Lifting myself up to a kneeling position, I remove the anal beads, slowly. Dragging them one by one until the last is free. When she groans, I smile down at her. Unlatching our feet, I allow her to fold forward before flipping onto her back. Peeling the final clamps off her breasts, I smile as she stares at me with desperate eyes. She loved what we did. She wants to tell me, but her arms and mouth are still under my control.

"What if I licked you for a while?" Dragging a finger through her arousal, her back arches. Her eyes tell me her answer is yes.

Peeling back her neatly trimmed lips, I hold her sex hostage. "Fuck, you're gorgeous everywhere, Siren." Muddling my fingers across her clit, Circe is ready for another round of bliss within seconds, and so am I. Arousing her is so easy. I've figured out what makes her tick. Wetting my lips in anticipation, I delve straight away to that peaked bud calling me. Taunting her for a moment, circling it, but not touching it, my own need arises again. Flicking, sucking, and pulling on it, laying my tongue flat, I relish her taste. Coursing across her sex from top to bottom, the shudder is felt in her legs when I reach a particularly sensitive spot. There won't be a drop left behind. She'll be dry when I'm done. Honestly, I can't get enough of her.

Seeing each other in person has been hard with our schedules, but when we're together, it's fireworks from minute one. Clothes are stripped and torn, bodies are entwined, and sleep is no longer a necessity.

"Love, I need more from you." Rising up, I unleash one of her hands from the manacles. Allowing her enough freedom to do what I want, she

pulls the gag off faster than I thought she could one-handed before she sits up. Lying sideways along the bed, her head is hanging off the edge. A grin dances across those fabulous lips. She knows what I want.

Moving off the bed so that I'm standing, I inspect my handiwork. I look at the red marks on her pert buds, the clamp indents, and the soft russet glow that appears on her cheeks. "So sweet. You know you have me addicted to you, Circe."

"Feeling is mutual, Wyatt."

Standing in front of her, leaning across her body, I flick her clit. "Take a deep breath, Siren." With her eyes dancing in anticipation, Circe wiggles her eyebrows at me. Placing my hardened cock into her open and inviting mouth, she draws in a sharp intake of air as her teeth lightly scrape the sides. Widening out, her open throat accepts my length gladly, tonguing the length of it.

Groaning, my body shudders. Dipping forward, sucking her greedy cunt, I feel the vibrations of her humming against my skin. Pulling at her already tortured bud, delving a finger within her ass and two within her sex, she pulls her mouth tighter against me. As her hands weave around to my ass, I feel her tug on the end of the rubber plug still situated. As she strokes it in time with her mouth, the tight motions almost unman me. Falling forward with a wicked abandon to feast on her body, I can't let this evening end. In less time than it takes to order room service, I'll be back with the race team in Daytona, while she'll be flying out to a LeMans in Monaco. It'll be weeks again before I see her. I need all the physical contact I can get to tide me over.

As cum flows freely, she falls apart for me all over again. Lapping it up, I feel every slight nip as she scrapes her teeth when her cheeks pull in. Pushing the plug in a bit further, Circe grips my cock at the base. Pumping deep within her hot mouth, I'm not sure how she's breathing. Feeling the air from her nose tickling against my ass, she presses her nails tightly to not only hold the plug in place, but to drag me even closer. Tighter than I thought I could handle, her one hand grips my shaft. Stroking it painfully,

I cry out my release. All reason is gone as I feel the end of my jettisoned release flowing down her throat. Even though I'm spent, I want to go again before she leaves me in just a few hours.

Lifting away from her mouth, I lay beside her on the bed. "Fuck, Siren. I'm done." Removing the plug myself, I lay it on the bed, beside the beads. Running a finger along her thigh, she lets out a deep giggle. It's not an "I'm funny," giggle, it's a "don't touch my over-sensitized body" giggle.

For sure, we'll be doing this again, and soon. I need as much as I can get. And no matter how many times I say I'm done and spent, it's a fucking lie. She's addictive.

Leaving that memory, reminding me it's not happening now, my prone body doesn't react. My mind is trying to save me by giving me great memories, allowing me to forget how fucked-up everything is. It's disconnecting me from the danger of reality. Sure, my conscious mind registers that I'm no longer in that memory, loving the woman that consumes my soul, but it's happier than the reality of being stuck here.

The fucked-up part of it? I'm not alone. It's a bit creepy that I'm thinking about sex with my girl while my baby sister sits vigil beside me.

As if she knows I'm conscious and can hear her, China speaks softly. "Wyatt, when you wake up, Jamieson, you, and I will have a massive convo about that day. I want to know it all. No, that's a fucking lie. I *need* to know what happened." My sister's voice pounds off the walls, the weight of it hitting me square in the chest. Her words hitch between heavy breaths. In a sick, twisted way, I'm glad I'm in my head. The sight of her crying would tear me apart. She has no idea what happened and what I went through that day. I'm not sure she could handle it all. The mixture of emotions are volatile — sadness, happiness, grief, despair, joy, despondency, anger, and peace. It's hard to express, and I'm not sure I could explain it coherently right now. Maybe the time in my head will help arrange it all.

What must she be thinking? China Crown is strong, daunting, and a banshee. Tears are not part of my sister's repertoire. What it must feel like to deal with death, destruction, and mayhem, without anyone to lean on. No one to talk to. I guess we're both alone right now. Yeah, Jamieson may be here, but Doll and I have always been close. We've been there for each other, and he's never been a part of her life.

"Wake up, please, Cas. Who'll race me? Who'll push me to be better? Dad..." Crying out the words in earnest, I feel her heart break. "I can't do this alone. Don't leave me." Her tight words break me.

With a light knock on the door, Doll sniffles, collecting herself before answering. "Come in," she calls out.

"CD? Can we come—" Peeking her head around the corner, standing in the light of the hallway, one of Doll's friends looks shocked. "Jesus fucking Christ on a cracker." Walking in, the shock is written on her face. Schooling her features, she steps in close. "Fucking hell, D."

"Yep. That about sums it up, Harlow." Rising out of the chair, she hugs Harlow. I feel better knowing she has someone here for her. "You alone, harlot?"

"Nope. The girls came too, but Hallette's arguing about the paperwork, and Cathryne's trying to get info from the nurse before she'll sign. Old biddy won't give up anything." Wrapping her arms around Doll, it breaks my heart to see her in pieces.

Standing there for a while, holding each other up, the other lunatics eventually join. Each are wide-eyed, their mouths gaping open as they take me in. If I didn't know before that I looked like shit, that my body was in a bad way, I do now. These three girls are not known for holding anything back in their assessments.

I think back on a day that myself and a few friends got into a toss-up with some kids at school. I'd come home with blood dripping out of my mouth, along with cuts, bruises, and torn clothes. We'd had our asses handed to us, and they didn't sugarcoat it. Since then, I've appreciated that the girls would always be honest with whatever they had to say. I know I have to look like I've been through a meat grinder, as that's how it feels.

"China..." Harlow looks at my prone and broken body, halting her thoughts, thinking of what to say. "He looks awful. I've seen bait dogs look better after a round."

"Can't disagree," Cathryne chimes in. "And you, Doll. You look like a cat that got stuck in a tree, lover. We need to get you to a shower, a clothing store, and a hairdresser."

Figuring out who's talking isn't hard, but after a bit, listening to their banter, I grow tired. Drifting back to sleep, the last thing I hear is their silly conversation about girl shit.

This will be good for Doll. She needed a break from being the *Queen of the Damaged*.

Chapter Nine

Circe

The doctor has ignored me time and again, doped me up over and over, then walked out, quickly stating an emergency with another patient. It could be a random patient, but I don't believe it is. It doesn't feel like it in my heart. More days have passed, and I can't even say how many it's been. I want to know *something*.

No. I *need* to know. I'm grateful for my life, but I need to know about them.

Is the emergency Wyatt?

Is it Marca?

Dr. Callie has forbidden the nurses and cleaning staff from handing me the remote or the paper. Softhearted pussies are fearful they'll spill the beans, so they avoid me.

Speaking of the devil in scrubs, Dr. Callie has been here for a good twenty minutes, looking over my damages for the day. I have enough energy now to stay awake beyond twenty minutes, and to speak a whole sentence without taking short breaths between words.

Reaching across, picking up a Styrofoam cup and the plastic jug from my side table, Dr. Callie pours me a cup of ice water. Handing it to me, with that same lamented look I've seen day after day, I smile.

"Thank you," I say, even though it's halfhearted. Taking the cup with my opposite hand, which is mighty tricky, I lift it to my parched lips and sip happily. These stupid drugs make me awfully thirsty. It's so bad, that I think I've drank my yearly ration of Californian clean water.

Pushing my hair back, peeling away the dressing that covers the stitches, she does her inspection. "Everything seems to be mending well on your forehead. I think that will clear up nicely."

"Do you have any idea when I might be allowed out of here, doc?" Reaching over, I shakily place the cup on the table. A week ago, that was an insurmountable feat.

"Until the rattle leaves your chest, you're staying put." Pressing the controls for the bed, Dr. Callie fluffs my pillow behind me, then raises the bed. "Is there anything you need today?"

"Nope. Nothing." I smile weakly, as it's such a wicked lie. She knows that, though. Dr. Callie's not a stupid woman, but evil for sure. I've tried on more than one occasion to trip her up and taunt her into giving me something, *anything*.

Looking over my paperwork once more, she leaves me alone to stew in my sadness. Once she's gone, I try to reach the side table that's just out of reach. I've tried this every day, and everyday I've given in and resigned myself to the fact that it takes more energy than I have. I'm animated today. I have an energy that I didn't have before.

Leaning out of the bed, and pulling the side table closer, it takes a great deal of effort. As my breathing hitches, I push past the pain. I'm not stopping until I've at least tried to learn the outcome of our crash. Having it in reach, flicking the portable receiver off the cradle, I bring the phone to the bed. Looking at it, trying to remember the combination of numbers, I get pissed. I can't remember anyone's phone number. Everything jumbles. One is something...4483? But I can't remember the area or zone codes. Punching in random sets of nothing feels right. After a moment of straining my already tired head, I give in and place the phone down on the bed.

Dialing the numbers I know so well on a cell is easy; pick the preset and go. Remembering a phone number isn't as simple. No amount of concentration can garner the digits I need either. "Fuck."

Not knowing or hearing about Wyatt, and not seeing him in person with an '*I'm okay*' is so hard.

Fate and love, I've learned, are intertwined. It was fate that changed my life, and it was love that crushed me, and both brought me to him. If my life hadn't changed all those years ago, I never would've been at that race. If fate hadn't intervened, would I have been at his caravan that day for the interview? No. It's been a short period of time, but I *know* my fate was tied to his. Would I even consider changing the past? Maybe, maybe not. It took me on a path that brought me to him. Even the heartache of what was taken in the past can't compare to what I've gained by being cared about, and caring deeply for Wyatt.

After a few exhausting minutes of despair, I decide to give up. I can't remember something as simple as phone numbers. Curling up to rest once more, a quiet knock on the door catches my attention.

"Hello?" I hear from the other side of the semi-closed door.

"Who are you looking for?" I ask.

"I'm looking for Circe? Circe Maco?" Without seeing the person's face, I *know.* It's the voice of someone I'd never forget in a million years.

How did she find me?

"I'm here."

Stepping around the curtain opening, I'm in awe of her consistent beauty. My mother was always a gorgeous woman. Her looks, her posture, her poise is all perfection. She's always been stunning, and I doubt she's aged a day. Gasping, she takes in my damaged body. I know what I look like. Wires, tubes, a lovely cast, and various nicks litter the surface of my skin with salve and bandages.

"I'm sure I look like shit. I feel like it for sure."

"Oh, darling. You look terrible." She pulls out the chair by the window, bringing herself closer to the side of the bed where my casted arm rests. "And I'm sorry, but you smell terrible."

"Since the accident, I haven't had a shower. It's been sponge baths. No privacy at all. All I want is a steaming, soaking-through-to-your-bones shower to remove the grime. And don't even start on the hair. I haven't seen a mirror. My doctor's kept me from looking to keep me calm. *Everything* is to keep me calm."

"I'm so glad you're okay, Circe."

"How did you know I was here?"

"It's all over the news."

Well, that's a blessing.

"Are they saying what happened? No one will tell me anything." Grimacing as a sharp pain lances through my side, I see the look on her face. It's that same one of pain I've seen more than I'd like. Is it because she thinks I'm in pain? Or that what she knows could be painful for me to hear?

"Circe. I was given strict instructions before entering—"

"Hold up. I haven't seen you in almost six years, and you won't tell me anything beyond what they have? Why are you here then?"

Her face falls as I cut her verbally. I'm sharp, sharper than she deserves. It's true, I haven't seen her, but that's not her fault. Not at all. "I'm a grown-ass fucking woman that can take a bit of mental anguish." Why I'm upset and crass is that everyone seems to think that they know what's best for *me*.

"Circe, I'm sorry for what's happened, but instructions are instructions when given by lawyers with confidentiality contracts." Sitting back against the chair, crossing her arms and lithe legs, she levels me with a look that states she's pondering how to address me next, so I wait. "Your father doesn't know I'm here. He knows you were in an accident, but he thought I shouldn't come. I could not let this go any further." The pain is visible in her sweet features. "I've missed you so."

Fuck. Now I feel like a little shit for the way I just acted. Do I feel bad about the way things went down all those years ago? Yes, but I can't change the past. I can only look to the future.

Unsure of how to answer her, I avoid the pain and the apology. "I'm tired." I roll over, onto my side. "I'm going to sleep."

"Do you mind if I wait here?"

Quietly, I say, "That would be fine. Thanks."

Chapter Ten

Circe
The Past

Lift. Lift. Lift!" Tamping her foot to the beat, smacking her hands together as she glares at me with a look of pure disgust, I lift higher. At least, as high as I possibly can.

"That's lazy, lazy, lazy. Do you want this or not, *paresse*?" Of course I do, I answer internally. Mentally, I'm critiquing my efforts, denying it's that bad of an attempt. I'm not a *sloth*, as she said, and my effort was exceptional. At least I think so.

"Pardon moi, Meme Léon." Stopping my spin, I saunter over to her. With a towel in hand, awaiting my open palm, I stop at the edge of the boards. "I will do better. I promise." Meme Léon is bundled up from top to bottom in a massive coat. Her hooked nose is the only thing showing outside her furry hood. Her record of attendance into the US Olympic program is one of the best.

This is all I've wanted. I've worked toward this point since I was five. Training at five thirty each morning with numerous personal coaches, trainers, and instructors, I'm preparing for the US Olympic Team. It's my dream. I've never slept-in a single day of my life. And even though I envy the kids that sleep until eight, eating a quick sugary breakfast of Fruit Loops or Cap'n Crunch, running out the door to classes with kids their own age, I doubt they have sports that eat up all their free time like I do. I doubt they're working toward the podium either, so there's that.

"Try it again. This time, I want to see lift." Turning away from me, as if I don't exist, she bends down and grabs her steaming cup of hot cocoa. Knowing I was dismissed, I skate off, back toward the starting point. I stand and await the control room to restart my music.

Scuffing the ice with my blades, shifting back and forth, I prepare. I love how the scraped surface leaves dusty clouds of white fluff in the air that sticks around the edges of my black skate boot. We've already been out here for three hours. Meme will keep me until my fingers are blue, and the air in my lungs is pure ice. I'll be here until I complete my quad jump properly. Trying over and over, I fail each time, landing hard on my ass. Feeling the blue-tinged bruise as it grows exponentially across my ass cheeks, I know I'll be so sore. For sure, I'm sleeping on my stomach.

Venturing a gander at her before my cue, Meme looks pissed. Watching the steam rise off her cup, she sips it. Staring me down, glaring dark daggers of hatred for keeping her here late, I prepare to impress her.

As the music starts its harsh melodic beat of drums, synthesizers and snares, my notes chime. Taking off like a shot, pounding my skates into the unforgiving ice, I glide back and forth across the surface. Gaining speed, I feel the same rush that comes to me each time I do this; I'm exhilarated and happy.

Timing is everything if I want to hit the corners exactly as I'm supposed to. Today, I've done this so many times that you'd think I should have this down pat, but I just keep fucking up that one jump. My arch nemesis, my quad axle. The routine has one quad, three triples, two doubles, a combo double - double, and one gloriously fun set of footwork.

Cutting deep into the ice, lifting the edge of the blade—and myself off the ground—I pound the end of my toe pick in launching myself forward and up. Swiveling and pushing myself to spin, I land with my outside raised leg straight. First jump down.

Turning around, pushing harder and harder, I advance into the middle of the arena. Feeling the icy air blow by my head, cooling me, I relish the breeze. The speed of it all, the sound of nothing but you and your blades cutting the surface gives you a rush. It's fucking heavenly.

Pulling in my left leg and gliding backwards, I look forward. Lifting from my right to spin forward, I turn twice in the air. Landing with ease, then picking my skate in once more, I add a second set of loops before pounding onto the ice again. Double-axle, double-loop, done.

When you know your efforts are what propelled you toward the next turn, the next set of footwork, or onto the next competition, it feels so good completing it. It's a rush of exponential proportions when your body does as its requested to do. This time, I hope it agrees to do as I mentally want.

The quad-axle has been the bane of my routine for over two weeks now—every morning, every afternoon, late into the night, and then restarting again. Every day I try, but fail at the quad. It evades me. It's the next jump, and I swear I'll land it, even if the landing is a bit dodgy.

Pulling through the footwork, I smile gleefully as it's my favorite part of any dance routine. You find yourself toe picking, gliding, skimming, turning back and forth, then doing it all over again in a seamless motion. Sure, the spins are great, and the jumps are okay, but I really love footwork. That's where your true talent shines through.

"Cut it deeper in the corner, Circe!" Meme yells out from the sideboards.

It wasn't tight enough for her, and I know I could have gone closer, but closer means I end up short on the other end of the landing. Ignoring her comment, I skate on. Last time she had me cut it deeper, I ended up in the boards with a sprained ankle and a week's bed rest.

Pushing harder and faster through the rest of the routine, pulling every bit of energy I have left, I see the prize. If I can land that quad, I'm going out tonight with friends, to a party. No, *the* party. Prom. Well, it's not necessarily my prom, as I'm homeschooled, but my best friends, Shelby and Kiresa, who live next door, invited me to come along with them. I want it so bad it hurts. A social life. Boys. A kiss. Hell, a stolen illegally absconded drink would be an utterly euphoric experience. But if I want it, I need to focus on the task at hand.

Tightening up my footwork and my speed before I venture into the middle of the rink, I hear Meme on the side shouting "Cut it. Cut it." I'm not listening because this feels so good, the way I'm going. I can make it. I can do this.

Prepping, I turn to see my visual landing. Releasing the coiled-up tension in my spin, I suck in a deep breath. As my foot hits the ice, I pull out my free leg and stick the landing perfectly. Skating off with a sense of freedom and joy in my accomplishment, I beam as I finish my routine.

Finally, I did it! I honestly did it! Sure, I'll have to prove it time and again before Regionals, or before she lets me prepare for the team, but I did it.

Ending my routine as the music stops, I head over to Meme. Seeing her scowling is not what I'd expected. Here I was, thinking she'd be proud me. Christ on a cracker, she's pissed. Without her blessing, I can't go tonight.

"I did it Meme Léon! I landed it clean."

"Oui, you completed it. Once, Circe. Do you understand that is not an accomplishment in success? Completing it multiple times is worth praise. Once is a fluke."

Well, that's a quick way to burst a girl's bubble. Thank. You. Meme.

Hanging my head, staring at the patchy snow piled against the boards, there's no more than a snowball's chance in Hades, she'll allow me to celebrate anything tonight, or any other night. Dammit.

For the next few moments she scolds me, reminding me of my failures, and that my single quad was not a measure of success. She then informs me the day is complete and I'm *allowed* to hit the shower. Tamping my blades on the hard floor, back to the changing area, I'm so upset at what a horrible day this has become. This is not a night of celebrating. No way will I be entertaining life as a regular teenager. I'll most definitely not be having that experimental time with a boy.

My life is controlled by others. When do I get a choice? My wants and needs are always overlooked, and it's becoming difficult to live with.

Cleaning up and clearing out of my private arena as quickly as possible, I find Meme Léon informing my highly strict and overprotective parents that I'm not deserving of a free night. *Thanks for crushing my hopes.*

Of course, that was after Shelby texted me that she'd snuck into my room.

S: It's there.

C: What is?

S: THE dress.

C: I can't.

S: See you at nine.

C: I won't be going. Have a great night.

S: I'll be there at NINE.

Informing me that the dress she left suited me best, I tried my best to ignore her. With or *without* permission, they'd be there to grab me. Great, another person to disappoint. I want so badly to go, but going against Meme's wishes will just cause me undue grief, further tightening of the leash, and a lack of free time with Shelby or Kiresa in the future.

Will it be worth it? Hell yes.

Will I do it? Probably not.

Getting back to the house a little over an hour ago, my father requested my presence. In his very formal and concise way, he said no. If Meme said no, then his answer was no.

Looking to my mother, sitting in her favorite wingback chair, legs crossed dutifully at the ankles, shoulders straight, and yet at ease, she's extravagant grace.

"No matter what I say, no matter how much I plead or beg, the answer will be no?"

"Please, understand. We know you want to take on the world as a bright and normal teenager, but I will reiterate. You, my sweetheart, are not a normal heathen like the rest of the rabble that attend those functions."

I'm done for. My father won't be swayed.

"Even if I promised more time on the ice, you'll still say no?" Attempting to look defeated and broken, I give my final attempt at changing their minds. Mustering all the sad pictures of hurt children, puppies, and washed up whales I can think of, I attempt tears. I've gotten pretty good at it over the years, and to be perfectly honest, I should be getting an Oscar for this next season. I'm that good.

"So that's it?" I say, hitching my breathing, allowing moisture to well in my eyes. "Nothing will change your minds on the matter?"

Looking at each other wordlessly, they shake their heads. The facade cracks slightly on my mother's perfectly demure face, but my father's stoic and stern gaze is still in place.

"No. I'm sorry. Olympic dreams come before a silly dance."

"Fine. I'll be in my room if you need me at all this evening." Turning heel to walk away, I add, "Actually, don't bother visiting. My door will be locked. I'll be unavailable. Have a good night." Smiling weakly, I kiss each of them on their outstretched cheeks before sauntering off to my room in the opposite wing from their sitting area.

Our house is so large and expansive, that for me to even speak to my parents face-to-face takes a good ten minutes from my side of the house to theirs. Really, I don't mind, as we have nothing in common. So many times, I've wondered if I was adopted, or the daughter of a long lost relative they took pity on. Then I look at them and myself. I see the uncanny resemblances reflected back, like in a mirror. The sharp cheekbones, the tight tiny freckles that are concentric. They're perfectly smattered all over the face of both myself and my father, as if we're carbon copies of each other.

My hair coloring and eyes are all my mother. Green like the sea foam that sprays up the coast near our beachfront, and coppery red strands, with soft strawberry highlights that neither of us have to pay for. Never mind the rail thin bodies we all have in common. Or the pianist fingers that hang like tree branches down our svelte forms. I lucked out on the metabolism of a house fly, with the appetite of a growing gorilla that keeps the kitchen hopping day and night.

When I finally make it back to my room, it's midday. The sun is crashing against the backdrop of the ocean outside my window, making me wistful. Despondently so. "Why are they so constricting? Why not allow me a bit of space so that I would feel freedom? Why make me feel like a prisoner to the sport I love?" Tossing off my sweater, I walk in and see the present from Shelby. "Fuck." Picking it up, turning it around and inspecting it in all its perfection, I'm more conflicted than before.

There's no way I'd stop skating just to gain the freedom I so desperately desire. I've invested too much of my childhood. The flip side to that coin is that I know I would give anything to be given the freedoms that other teenagers in my position are granted.

It's unfair that I have anything I could want or need, but the true price of freedom is immeasurable to me.

Whether I had permission or not, Shelby and Kiresa would be coming at nine. They'll push me into it whether I like it or not. The beautiful dress eggs me on to defy my parents, and if I have any chance at keeping the only friends I hold dear, I'll find a way to escape, undetected.

Smelling like a sweaty gym room after a team of boys have returned, another shower is key. My hair is in shambles—ratty and tangled from all the exertion, even after a shower at the rink. And if I want to look presentable in that dress, I better shave. Stinky girls with wisps under their arms most definitely don't get a kiss from the prince.

A few hours later, pacing the room has done nothing to help me make a definitive decision. I tried a list of pros and cons, a coin toss. I even put the dress on and stood in front of the mirror, imagining myself dancing with a hot guy named Jackson, Kendrick or even a Phillip. It fit like silk. Dealing with my parents and Meme...will it be worth the pain and anguish they'll impart for defying them? Mostly. But if I don't try to be a rebellious teenager that would put myself out there and do as I pleased without permission, then have I really lived?

"Shit. How much of a wuss am I?" I'm a straight A student. I do all the tasks set forth, and I'm prepping for my first year at college without stepping foot outside our mansion. I *need* to do this for my own sanity.

Shelby and Kiresa have texted me nonstop since two thirty.

Kiresa: *Are you?*

Shelby: *Did they?*

And the occasional *So???* from both.

Pinging back and forth between us, my phone is running out of juice. Finally breaking free, I answered their hundredth question.

Me: *I'm going.*

Parents and Meme be damned. I want out of this house. I'll enjoy an evening without the restraint of being a modest and obedient person. I'm almost eighteen. I think I'm old enough to decide if I want something more than being a prisoner to their choices. Yet I'm still young enough to be scared shitless of their reprimands.

With the dress on, hair done, makeup pristinely applied with a touch of harlot,

I'm ready to break free.

Chapter Eleven

Circe
The Past

Receiving a text from Kiresa that they were on the way over, I was anxious, nervous, and excitedly prepared to say the least. Moving to the sundeck of my room where the door opens up to the grounds, I gather my clutch, phone, and a lip gloss, in case I need to repair my look throughout the evening. As I'm stepping out, my phone rings. It's my mother.

"Hello?" I don't know if she can hear my trepidation or fear, but I hope to hell I don't garner any attention. I don't want her to feel she needs to visit my side of the house.

"Darling. Your father and I have talked again about the circumstances from today..." She pauses. As she paces back and forth, I can hear her heels clicking on the Italian tiles in her room. "I'm sorry you feel we aren't giving you a fair shot at living your teenage life. Your studies and lessons must come first if you are to receive any Olympic invitations."

She's probably had an in-depth conversation with my father about allowing me to go, and his answer never changed. She's the softer of the two. I can usually count on her siding with me, and I'd really hoped she would. Unfortunately, I think she agreed wholeheartedly with him.

"I get it, Mom. If I want to be the best, I need to give the best I have. It just sucks I have to give up being independent and adventurous at the same time." I slowly close the doors of my patio, exiting into the moonlit night. "Don't worry about me. I have to get up extra early anyway. Meme wants me at the rink at five am. I probably won't see you until after lessons."

She's stopped moving, probably sitting in her favorite lounger off her en suite. "I love you, Circe. I just want the best for you. Taking the high road instead of arguing the point further shows your character. I'm proud of you."

Fuck. Way to make me feel worse about what I'm doing. "I know, Mom. I'm gonna go, okay?" Closing the door, it clicks silently.

"Night, Circe. I love you."

"I love you too." Hanging up the line, placing my phone in my clutch, I feel like a horrible daughter.

Moving down the side of the house and hopping into the waiting car, Kiresa is first to pipe up. "Your parents said no. And you, Circe, are still doing it?"

"I really need you to start the car before security notices something."

"Circe, you never defy your parents," Shelby says over her shoulder as we drive down the long winding road toward the city.

"I defy them. I just do it in my own way."

"You kill them with kindness? Or is it that silence is golden?" Kiresa's smirk is gleeful.

"You know it's going to cost you, right?" Shelby pipes in, bringing the car to a stop at the light. Turning on her blinker, we wait for the red light to change. Turning, she glares at me with that knowing smirk, the one that tells me not only will I pay for this from *them*, but also because I defied my parents. She now knows she can make me do it on a whim with a wink, a nudge, and a pretty dress.

"Yes. I know you're going to use this as ammo for the next time you get me to break the rules." Picturing the next insane act of defiance that she'll think up, I shake my head and smile. Bungee jumping? Sky diving? Maybe racing. Or she'll have me speed dating with older men. This could be dangerous.

"Shel, light's green." We head down the freeway toward the hotel.

"I can't be out past twelve or I'll be a wreck for tomorrow's training. If I can't land that quad again, I won't be off the ice until I'm an old hag." As they both laugh, giving me no answer about the curfew, I know this will be a dangerous night. I'm not entirely sure if it's because they doubt I'll be on time, or if they think it's funny I'm setting us one. Either way, I hope they take me seriously.

There's a ton of traffic tonight on the freeway as we hop on the express toward Venice Beach. One of the girls, Joanie so-and-so, her parents own this massive hotel. They gave her the run of the high-end palace for the weekend, and I can see danger looming in the near future for many. Probably a police officer or two as well.

"BTW, Circe. I did tell you that dress was vintage, right?" Kiresa informs me.

"Vintage, huh? I didn't know that." I smile weakly.

Shelby merges into the next lane like a boss, making it look so easy. I envy her. I haven't even had a chance to drive. Skating has taken up too much time to allow me any moments behind the wheel.

"Circe, can you pass me my lip gloss? It's in my bag on the seat beside you." Deciding when I got in to sit in the middle, I reach into her clutch and pull out the gloss. The last thing I wanted to do was wrinkle the dress with the chest seatbelt. Leaning forward to be within their conversations, I hand up the small tube.

That's when there's an ear-splitting shriek and a peeling noise, like metal being pulled apart. It's unlike anything I've ever heard before. As the sky falls, the ground comes up to greet me. My head bounces off the seat where my friends are. I feel like a pinball. It's jolting and jarring as my teeth rattle against each other, causing me to nip my cheeks numerous times before I pass out.

Coming to, I find it hard to comprehend the carnage. Shelby's head sits at an unnatural angle against the dash, lying by the radio. A song pipes through the speakers still, wailing about a party. Blood slicks the screen and debris surrounds us. Kiresa is leaning against the bare ground. Her window is shattered into a thousand pieces as blood pools around her tangled and dirty platinum hair. Seeing her body hung up in the window frame as we lay sideways in Shelby's mangled Mercedes, I know this isn't good.

I move. I need to make sure my friends are alive.

"Shelby, can you hear me? Kiresa?" Neither answer. Not a moan, not a groan. Nothing.

I try to remove my seatbelt, but it won't budge. It's stuck. With my face pushed up against the seat tightly, I lean in to reach Kiresa. Hanging sideways, pulling myself forward on her seat, she's far enough away I can only just reach her. Feeling for a pulse, I expect movement on her skin, but there's none.

Fuck, fuck, fuck.

There's no chance Shelby's alive, not with her head at that angle, but I feel for her pulse anyway. She's like loose rubber, bendy and soft. Touching her neck gently, near the spine, it's crunchy feeling. Both of them are dead, I know it.

"Hello? Are you okay in there?" I hear someone call out. They're not right beside the car, but they're close.

"In here!" Yelling back, my voice cracks as I begin to cry.

There's scrambling against the underside of the car, like someone's trying to scale their way to my door. A man, about twenty years old or so, peers through the top of the smashed window.

With a smile, he looks down at the girls. "How are you? How are your friends?" he asks as he tries to hold onto the door and open it at the same time, breathing heavily.

Sighing, I can't say it yet. If I answer that they're dead, then it becomes true. "My ears are ringing and my head hurts." I yank on the edge of my strap. "And my belt's stuck."

"Hold still," he says. "Let me get the door open." Jerking hard, he yanks on the door until it swings free, upward and away.

"Let me see if I can get you out, then we'll get your friends."

Leaning in, so that his body hangs upside down inside, he's suspended by his torso. "I'm Jack. And you are?" A wicked grin paints his features.

"Circe." I'm trying to work the buckle, but it won't budge.

"Well, Circe. Let's see if we can't get you free. Move your hand away from the side. I'm going to cut the strap." Scooching my butt over a bit, gravity pulls my body away from the seat belt strap. Pulling out a tool, Jack runs it along the belt a few times until I hear a pop, and feel a lack of tension.

"Can you move, Circe? I'd hate to see you stuck after all this work." He winks. Like, actually winks, then smiles once more. It's an electric grin.

"Are you hitting on me while trying to play the hero, Jack?"

"Nope." Again with that smile. "I'm just trying to occupy your mind. You need to keep calm, and if a smile does it, I'll keep doing it," he grunts. "Hold on a second, okay? I'm just turning around."

Jack disappears, and as I feel the car shift, his feet appear. Dangling close to where my face is, perching himself, he holds onto the edge of the driver's seat for support. "Okay, Circe. When I say I need you to let go of the seat, wiggle your legs. We'll get you out of here so we can look after your friends, all right?" Nodding, I reach for his hands, one at a time.

"Here we go," he says, very controlled. "On the count of three, I'm going to pull you up. I need you to use your feet to rise. Use the back of the seat as a ledge to lift yourself up." He leans forward until I can grip his hands tightly.

"One. Two." I prep myself for the jolt when he pulls. "Three." I lift my left leg to rest it on the headrest.

"That's good, Circe. Now, the other leg." I look down to my feet and where I need to put my other leg. It's right by Kiresa's head, or rather, where Kiresa's head should be. She should be leaning on the headrest, laughing, joking, smiling at me, and winking at this good looking older guy helping us.

Taking a deep breath, pulling in my courage, I attempt to lift my right leg. It doesn't move.

"Circe, I need you to put that other leg up. Can you put it up there, please?"

"I—I can't, Jack. I can't seem to lift my leg." My voice sounds shaky and warbled.

That's when I freak out. Like, truly, fully, unbelievably freak out. My pulse is racing. My heart feels like it will jackhammer out of my chest, and I *can't* move my right leg.

"Circe, I need you to stay with me. Work with me. We'll get you out of here, okay? Help me with getting you out." Jack sees the panic and fear in my face as he's trying to keep me upright. If I fall now, I'll be against the window frame, lying in a pool of Kiresa's blood with shards of broken glass.

"Look, there's no turning back." Jack's voice is very commanding, and he makes me turn to him. "I'll pull you up, but you have to help by lifting as well. I *can't* do it all."

Breathing deep, I look up at Jack's cool, calm, greyish eyes to answer. "Okay, let's go."

Nodding, he pulls me up. As I lift off from the headrest with my left, together we pull me out the open door. Other people have now gathered. They too are helping lift me out of the wreckage, laying me on the ground below.

A makeshift pallet has been setup with a grey blanket someone has placed on the pavement, along with a first aid kit and flares that are lit on either side of the car. People are scrambling everywhere, panicked. With help, I sit down on the blanket, stretching out my right leg. The bone is broken right above my knee, causing it to rest abnormally. There's no feeling in it. Either shock or adrenaline is rushing through me, as I'm numb to the pain.

Watching Jack disappear a few more times into the car to check on Shelby and Kiresa, he'll find exactly what I already know, and it frightens me.

Why am I alive?

Pulling up a seat beside me on the ground, the sullen face of Jack makes it apparent. Everything is different now. I take a look around at the carnage, and the shocked and scared faces that surround me. I don't know what's going on, and I was there. Some even ignore me, hopping back into their cars as they try to erase the pall of death they've just viewed. Losing two friends...I can't erase that.

The cops will call Shelby and Kiresa's parents, telling them about the accident and their deaths, all as I'll be on the way to a hospital, without my parents knowing I was even out.

OH.MY.GOD! My parents have no idea I'm here. They'll get a call in the middle of the night that their daughter was in an accident, that someone died. They're going to freak.

"Um, Jack? Do you have a phone I can use to call my parents?" Turning, he reaches into his pocket and hands me his cell.

Dialing, it rings a few times before the first click.

"John Matcheson, speaking...Hello? Who is this?" He sounds groggy. He must have been asleep.

"Daddy, it's me." Tears start to flow down my cheeks.

"Circe?"

"Yeah. I, um, I need your help."

"I don't understand? Whose phone are you calling from?" He sounds perturbed.

"I've been in an accident with Shelby and Kiresa." No matter the outcome, I know this won't go well. My parents will be so upset, so disappointed in me.

"Circe. It's ten thirty. Where are you, sweetheart?"

"We were on the Interstate, and I'm just waiting on the ambulance to package me up."

His voice is tight, stern, and fearful. "What hospital are they taking you to?" Weighing heavy in the pit of my stomach, I feel the dread of it in his voice. My father's not afraid of anything.

Pulling the phone away, I turn to Jack. "What hospital will they be taking me to?"

"UCLA, I believe."

Placing the phone back to my ear, I hear my father's reply. "I heard him, dear. Your mother and I will meet you there shortly." There's a pause on the line before he speaks. "Are you safe for now, Circe?"

"Yes." I pull the rough blanket closer to my chest. It's a warm night, but I feel chilled. Death walked across my soul.

"We'll see you shortly." With that, my father hangs up.

I pass it back to Jack. "Thanks for that. Actually, thank you for everything, Jack." Trying to smile only starts a heavy round of tears.

Chapter Twelve

Wyatt

Constantly looping.

Ever the same, over and over.

Every dream, every ambition. Every moment in time repeating, again and again. Everything.

The day I met her, the day we first fucked, the days surrounding Dad's funeral, and all the times leading up to this current disaster.

Fuckin' depression eats me alive. Circe cared for me unlike anyone has, coddling me as I wept like a heartbroken soul. She's always there in every thought, in every silent moment I'm alone here. The need for her at this desperate time is heady. Calling to me, my goddess brings me back from the brink, reminding me I can do this, that I can survive this latest curveball. In every thought that consumes me, showing me that I can be a better person, that I can find a better way to deal with the pressure of not being enough, she's there. Circe.

Circe saw the pain of it. She knew that being there was enough, enough to help me survive this internal war. It feels like I'm tied to a chair with rough cords, with a massive overhead light shining down as I'm being interrogated by my own defective mind.

The day's blend as the drugs cause me to constantly feel awake, yet asleep. I ghost through the memories of my past. I want to wake, but I've overheard the nurse, the doctor, and Doll chatter on about my condition. My swelling is not coming down as they'd hoped. They're certain a few more days should help before they wean me, pulling me from the coma. They have no idea what they've subjected me to. My tainted mind is the most dangerous place on earth. They shoved me inside it, locking it behind as they tossed away the proverbial key. I feel more trapped than ever.

The good I can find from this? I have an opportunity to go back through everything and slot the pieces that fit. The pieces that are incorrectly placed in my psyche will be erased, obliterated, removed and destroyed. When I *do* wake up, I will work free of the drugs that were prescribed to help with the depression and mood swings. A lot of it was created by triggers.

The trigger.

The major trigger is gone. That, I'll deal with later.

Dealing with family matters seem to be an ongoing disaster. With Dad, with our crash, and the will. When I wake up, there will be lawyers with paperwork, perched on a tree branch like vultures. Respecting the position they've given me is one thing, accepting it is another. I don't know how to be what they want—what it *takes*. This will change my life in ways I can't fathom.

Laying here, day after day, unable to do much of anything else, I think of my past—*our* past. Remembering the first night we met, my mind wanders through bright points. It wasn't love at first sight for either of us. Fuck. I pissed her off and I couldn't drink in enough of her sassy attitude. *Yes*, it's only been months, and *yes,* I know my manic depression can make my need for others constricting, but Circe has dealt with my quirks in stride. She's made me feel better about it all.

Envisioning her, my mind reels in every nuance of her look. The slight rose tint in her cheeks that softens her look, but in no way diminishes those pouty full lips that taper to a tiny, dimpled chin. Her sea foam, stormy green eyes that are perfectly spaced between the most adorable freckles. All of that rests atop her long slender neck. The things I've thought about doing to that neck and those pouty lips should be illegal. The things I've done and intend to do again as well. Her parents named her aptly. Daily, she's a Siren, calling me to my redemption.

Fuck, there's no lying to myself. She's been a distraction, but the right one. I'd say my head wasn't in the races, but I still came out on top and it worked out. Fuck anyone who wants her out of my life.

After Dad's death, Mother didn't want her around. Her sharp tongue and crass demeanor made it very clear that Circe was, in her opinion, the wrong thing for me. She felt that Circe was only after our money. I didn't think it was her business, so I never told her of Circe's past or her family. On the day of the crash, Mother and I, we'd had a heart to heart. She was still oblivious about Circe. Maybe I'd feel less guilt if she knew?

Maybe it makes no difference?

Either way, everything moved so fast those first few weeks. All I wanted was her with me. If it wasn't on a phone, it was in person. My cell was on constant charge from the texting and video calls, and I've spent a fucking fortune to have her flown out at a moment's notice to see me all over the globe.

I remember the weeks after Dad's very public funeral with sweet regard. Whiskey had gone back to Colorado. He was done with *family*. Yeah, he came for the funeral and left right after, but I couldn't get him on the phone for love or money, and the lawyers told me he must be present. Fucking pricks. It's bad enough I don't want the job. Jamieson will want what's expected of him even less. So of course, someone had to get him to come back to California for the mandatory reading of the will, and it sure as shit wasn't going to be mother.

Calling up his team manager, our Aunt Janie, I let her know I'd be stopping out to talk. Thankfully, she answered, telling him to expect me.

Getting to Vale, I got in early enough to watch one of Whiskey's races. It was the first time Circe had seen something of Whiskey's, and she was impressed. She was totally enthralled by the whole pantomime of snowboarding races, half-pipe competitions and freestyle jumps. Her eyes were alight with joy.

Afterwards, the three of us had dinner. We talked about everything, and he promised to fly out the night before the reading of the will. Whether we liked it or not, it was a necessity. The best part, he and Circe hit it off pretty quickly. And yeah, I didn't need his approval, but it felt nice.

When he up and left us before dessert, chasing tail, I had a dirty thought. Circe jumped on it immediately with excitement and an itching anticipation. Watching her floating ethereally toward the bar, stopping right beside a man about our age, I sit in a quiet corner of the bar. Circe selects the seat beside him, hoping to engage his attention. I have to admit, I didn't expect that I'd like it, watching him check out what is mine and mine alone. It both angers and arouses me. But it's a game I'm willing to play, as long as it's harmless.

Wearing a light peach dress, fluttering in the night breeze, Circe's a contrast to the dark and dangerous girls here. Each of them are looking to hook up with the guys here for one single night, nothing permanent, except for STDs or a stolen wallet. It makes Circe a sweet, delectable angel to the dark devils surrounding her. She's amazing and perfect in every way.

Yeah, maybe I have no right to someone like her. I'd broken her, destroyed her. She will never be the same innocent girl I met, and that turns me on. From where I sit, I can smell her perfume, and wanting to touch that soft skin so badly, it makes my cock engage in ways I can't voice. To fucking own her body and soul every night is my only goal.

Pulling up a chair beside the man, he takes in her beauty, then offers her a drink, of which she gladly accepts. Watching them interact, I keep a close eye on her. It may be a game, but it's *our* game, and the last thing I need is someone getting palmy with what is mine.

Receiving her drink, I see that something's off. The way the bartender looks to the man for approval, the way they signal each other, as if it's a scam, leads me to believe that her drink has been spiked. Carefully observing every movement, every nuance of him, I watch her take a sip of the concoction. If it's spiked, it won't take long for her to become incapacitated and pliable. The perfect toy for his intentions.

As they converse, she continues to engage him. Her movements become sluiced, awkward and vulcanized. It's easy to see that she's been drugged. Scanning the bar, looking for me, I understand the feeling well. Having a loss of control is daunting and fucking scary when you don't expect it.

Immediately, I rise from the chair, feeling the steam building within. Something I haven't done recently is let my darker side loose. I actually relish it in a way sometimes.

When I'm near enough to kiss her cheek, I dip my head in close. "Darling, it's time for bed."

Turning, her eyes are like saucers, and she can't respond. My chest tightens. My breathing shortens considerably, and the anger fuels my need to tear him apart. He's not about to get what he wanted from her. *His* need was to fuck her into next Sunday.

"Who are you, buddy?" The date rape druggist asks.

Turning, I punch him square in the jaw before he has a moment to comprehend the situation. As soon as his ass hits the floor, my fists drive into his cheek and teeth, over and over. Yes, I may enjoy sex as a release, but letting out my inner demon on a piece of shit like him is far more fun.

"You piece of fucking garbage!" I lay into him repeatedly. It's easy to see he isn't used to giving or receiving abuse. His hands cover his face, and he tries to curl up on the floor in a fetal position. Once I feel he's suffered enough, I release the collar of his cheap suit, allowing him to flop unconscious to the dirty carpet. Inspecting his wallet, there isn't much there. Pulling out his driver's license, it's just as I'd suspected. He's the worst kind of fucking garbage. A man with a family at home, and more than likely, a frequent proclivity for doing this to women when he's on the road.

Rising off the floor, I turn to the bartender. His back is squarely against the back bar. "Did you call the cops?" I ask him.

"Fuck yeah. Of course, I did."

"Good."

Circe starts to sway. "Wyatt?"

"You're okay, Siren. Just sit there." I turn back to the bartender. "Hand me a glass and your spout. I'll pour the glass. After that, don't touch a fucking thing." Frightened, he nods as he hands me a glass, then shows me the water button on the filler. "Don't think I won't climb over that bar and make you pay too."

I place the glass in her hand. "Siren, drink this. It'll help." As she sips it slowly, I do my best to keep her awake. She'll need the water to flush her system out, and to not have a drug hangover in the morning.

While I'm worrying over her, the cops walk in. With demands and questions, the patrons of the bar point to me as the culprit. I was more than happy to give them my statement. In the end, the bartender and the salesman were both carted off. One bloody, and one that got off lucky.

The whole ordeal took less than an hour. Lifting herself off the stool, slowly, I direct her, my mind still pulsing with rage. "Love, it's time to go." The once rubber movements have lessened, and became more controlled. It will still be hours yet before she's back to normal, but I feel good. Those two won't be able to do this to other defenseless women in the future.

I gather my calm, thinking of nothing but caring for her. "Let's not do that again. Okay, Siren?"

Tonight, I'll be caring for her, and in the morning, I'll show her body just what she means to me.

Circe Maco is someone I never intended to find. And in my future, I want more of everything she has to offer. I have chills of anticipation, thinking of our lives together. Figuring out what makes her tick, having those fuckable lips wrapped around my cock until they're swollen every morning and night—that's what I want.

Wishing that I was sucking and licking every inch of her body, consuming her mind—these are the pieces of her that I *need* now.

Nothing more will satisfy me.

Chapter Thirteen

China

Beep. Beep. Beeeeeeeeeep. The monitor chimes.

"Wyatt?" I check his breathing. "No. No, no, no. You're not doing this to me! Wyatt!"

Hanging over the edge of the bed, shaking him, I try to rouse him, yelling out his name until the nurses run in.

"China, step back," Nurse Sali tells me. Pulling at my shoulders, she drags me from my brother. I know she's doing it to help, but I swear, if the last thing I do with my brother is watch him die...I won't survive it.

Stepping back from the bed, doing as I'm told, Sali checks the monitors, checks Wyatt, then hits the button on the wall. As an alarm rings out on his monitors, extra nurses run in surrounding him. I'm not sure what they're doing, but as long as he's alive, I don't give a fuck.

"Shit, we're losing him again!" Over the hospital speakers, the sounds of 'Code Blue' and our room number repeats. I slowly become numb to the activity.

"Get the crash cart. Call Dr. Callie, now!"

Chapter Fourteen

China

"Code blue, room four-fifty-two. Code blue, room four-fifty-two." I'm watching my brother code.

"Miss Crown, please, move to the side for us." Everyone scrambles in, shoving the chair and the bed I've been on so they can lower Wyatt's bed to a flattened position.

Shoving myself into a corner, I give them as much room as they need as I watch them perform chest compressions over his heart. Yelling orders, telling others to move, I blank out. Their attempt to bring my brother back from the brink of wherever it is he's gone is all that matters. Has he ventured off to a dream? Slid off into a nightmare that's constricting his soul? I don't know. I don't care.

Curling into a ball against the wall, I vacantly take in all that they do. I could never explain what it feels like to watch this act, this dance of life and death, but I can't turn away. Fearing that if I pull my eyes from him, he'll try to escape, leaving me here alone. There's *no one* that could tear me away from this.

"Clear!" Dr. Callie yells as everyone backs away. Wyatt's body bows, jerking back against the stark bed frame as everyone holds their positions. Gazing at the monitor that's continued to squeal, nothing changes. "Reset," she says to the nurse rubbing the paddles together.

"Charging." As the doctor ventures a look my way, I try to remain calm.

Everyone waits patiently as the system sets up before she says again, "Clear!" She hits his body once more. His body jolts after she touches the paddles to his body, and I feel every ounce of the electricity as it courses through him. I'd do everything I could to remove his pain, but him leaving me now is not an option.

"Come on, Wyatt. Don't leave me," I say quietly to myself. Rocking back and forth, I remind myself to breathe. Nipping the insides of my mouth to almost bleeding, I hold my breath until the monitor starts to beep out a consistent rhythm, ending the cruel beep.

Placing the paddles to the side, Dr. Callie thanks everyone and places the blanket back across my brother's chest. They all clear out quietly and orderly as I track the beeps. One, two, *beep*. One, two, *beep*. One, two, *beep*. The sound holds me hostage. I have no understanding of its need, other than it means my brother is here and I'm not alone.

Bending down, Dr. Callie places her hands on my knees, "He's still here, China."

Pulling my gaze from Wyatt feels wrong, but I give the doctor a split second of my time as I respond. "Thank you."

"Always. It's what I'm here for, darlin'."

Chapter Fifteen

Wyatt

Days upon days. Hours tick down slowly. Minutes seem eternal. Watching, waiting for someone, *anyone*, to speak to me directly is excruciating.

Walking in, both the doctor and the nurse offer to get my sister anything she may need. I truly appreciate it. Knowing that others are there for her eases my mind a little. Trusting that Doll can handle everything tossed at her is a pipe dream. Sure, she's evil on a track, but she's so young, and we've lost so much lately.

Whiskey arrived at some point, and I've seen him taking care of her in his own way. His grumbly conversations are subdued. His usual stark demeanor is calm, and even though he's pacing like a caged animal, I know he's here to help. Her posse of bandits have been in and out too, feeding her, giving her moral support, and keeping her from taking all of this too deeply. They're helping her cope.

Myself? How am I handling this? Not well.

Every time I think I get a handle on the silence in my own head, Doll and Whiskey fall out of focus, their words blur and my mind blanks. Staring down a dark tunnel, where there's no one and nothing, is the wrong place for me. My illness—if that's what you call it—strangles me. There's no sound, and no one to talk me down from the silent musings of pain and anguish. No one to argue with either. It reminds me that even though my mother was my greatest trigger, she was also what made me notice I was alive. Yes, we fought, but she had her reasons behind all that she did. Did I despise her for it? Obviously. But with great regret. I take comfort in that last day.

Remembering when everything truly took a turn for the worst in our family, the bane of our arguments comes to mind freely. That day turned my fate.

"Wyatt! Are you coming?" She yells down the hall.

"Not even close, Mother," I mutter to myself. Fuck, do I wish I were. We're off to have a rare meeting at the table in the grand salon, as mother calls it, to speak of business. Our family is in one place. All of us are together, which is not something that's easily done.

Whiskey flew in this morning and he already looks ready to tear this place apart. It's mid-July. With the sun streaming in, heating every surface, it's definitely not his favorite place to be. Doll is still just a kid, and she really has no choice in the matter. I've only just turned twenty, and it's inevitable that I'm included in this soiree whether I like it or not. We're puppets in the Crown play, and each of us has our part to play in the future.

Popping into the room, Mother sits on the far side, opposite our team of lawyers. Dad is at the head of the table, while Whiskey is pacing the room. He's awaiting me and the end to this infernal crap.

"Thank you for giving us a moment of your time, Wyatt." Mother signals the seat beside her, expecting me to accept.

As if mud is stuck to the roof of my mouth, I take a seat and avoid the fight that she's looking for, for now.

Pulling out a chair, two down from her, I sidle up to Doll. Her and I would rather hit the track today. Dad has a race in less than twenty-four hours, so you can see each of our minds are elsewhere. His is practicing turns, thinking in moments of throttle position and drag coefficients. Ours is trying out new programming on the bikes. It's supposed to give us a five second advantage, and I'm itching to try it.

Huffing out a deep breath, Mother begins. "Margo, Merconda, and Jack, thank you for coming over today to go over this with the whole family. There's no use in doing it more than once. If you could begin, I'm sure that my children will be quiet listeners."

Great. She's already nipping at our heels, and the gathering hasn't even begun. Doll knows me, knows how this riles up my need to snap back. Touching my hand lightly, tapping it, she's telling me to be patient. Smiling her way, I nod.

Noticing that we're all being quiet and acquiescent children, Merconda starts. "Well, thank you for giving us the floor, Mrs. Crown. I'll try to keep it short. If there are any questions, I'm sure we can tackle them after." Pulling out stacks of pinned sheets, she hands them to Margo and Jack, who then move around the table, setting a clipped set in front of each family member, along with a shiny new Mont Blanc. "As per the request of your parents, their wills have been recently adjusted. Please read over the leaflets, and sign the appropriate positions noted by the tabs."

"This isn't right, Mother. You've given us no time to decide if this is right for us. What if I don't want to sign it?" My brother doesn't even open the paperwork. Slamming the pen that he was handed down, he rises from his chair and starts for the door.

"Son. Sit." Dad's voice is commanding, halting Whiskey's exit. Normally, he's the one in the background, quietly voicing opinions, awaiting us to decide our own courses. For him to speak out harshly to Whiskey is unusual.

"I'm not up for this bullshit. Why should I sit here and wait? It's inevitable that I'll be excluded." Straining his teeth, you can almost hear the enamel scrubbing off as he stands there, visibly stressed.

"Whiskey. Sit, please." Dad says it this time with a dark intent, but in his quiet calm.

Nodding to Dad, he slowly pulls the chair back and sits, but it's not restful. Pulling air through his teeth, crossing his arms tightly, you can see he's ready to bolt at a moment's notice.

"Could we continue?" Charming, yet crassly, Merconda peers at Jamieson over the top of her wire rimmed glasses, with a scowl of disgust. "So, as I already stated, your parents have adjusted their wills. The original format was to leave it to you each in trust until you became twenty-five. Seeing that Jamieson has almost reached that age, and is not involved in Crown Industries in any way, being that he is immersed in his own affairs, it has been corrected." Turning her sights from

Jamieson, she focuses on me. "Wyatt, if you could. Please turn to page seventy-two."

The shock must be blazing its way across my face as Doll squeezes my hand in a show of solidarity. Looking down the length of the large table to my brother, I'm shocked. He never felt that mother would continue the original format, passing it along to him, the snow racer, but to remove it from him just as he reaches his birthday is a serious asshole move.

Looking to Dad, his face is sullen and alight with stress. It shows his displeasure at this turn of events. No, I never assumed it would stay as it was, but to do this is unfair.

"You both felt it best to do this now? Why?"

Not allowing Dad to answer, Mother chimes in quickly. "Well, Wyatt. You do have your faults, your moments that cause me great displeasure and disgust, but in all those moments, I still see you as the rightful heir to the position." Fuck. I knew she'd go there eventually.

Tossing the paperwork across the table, Whiskey narrowly misses Margo's head. "You're kidding me!" Pushing the chair tightly back against the wall, flames can be seen in Whiskey's eyes. "Dad, I love you. Cas and Doll, I'll see you if you call me, but otherwise, I'm out of this family."

He glares at mother. "Don't call. Don't ask for me to pop over for family meetings, dinners, occasions, or celebrations. I was never a Crown to you. Thank you for reminding me of that." Storming out of the room, feeling the heat rise off his body, Whiskey passes us, slamming the salon doors behind him.

"Was that really necessary?" Merconda asks, slightly miffed that a show of emotion was brought into a very analytical affair. Showing her disdain at our family squabble, I can't believe her audacity. Her lack of care or compassion is why she's Mother's lawyer.

"Are you fucking kidding me? Are you really that callous? You're a fucking—"

"Wyatt!" Raising her voice, spitting mad, Mother interrupts me at the worst time.

"Don't act like this wasn't all your doing." Rising from my chair, I move toward my parents, seeing red.

"Cas, don't let her—"

"Doll. Don't be a silly girl. She's pitted us against each other, changing our fates. We haven't even been told the worst parts yet, I'm sure? I doubt you or I will be content with the direction they've chosen."

"Casper, your mother and I felt it best to leave the team in better hands. Someone who would run it correctly. Someone who would perform as tasked, that would benefit the team." Dad truly feels he's made a move that will be best for the team, for the family and for the future. I disagree. I look over at Mother, who's chomping at the bit to throw us into chaos. Dad holds her hand, slowly calming her down, even as that glint of trouble lights her features. He has a way with her, just as Doll has with me.

Standing beside me, Doll is hoping I won't cause a scene, that I won't need to be subdued.

Calming myself slightly, listening to his words, it sounds as if he's decided we're best split up, going our separate ways in business overall. Taking in what he suggests, I sit back down, even though I don't feel I should. "Do you really feel this is best? I don't see this as a way to keep us whole."

My father shakes his head. "Wyatt, please read the forms. When you're done, argue your points. At least give your sister the opportunity to see what is required of both of you."

Hating to disappoint him, I do as he instructs. Blowing out the fire that is banked within me, I gather serenity from every cell I own and slightly relax, waiting to hear them out.

"Thank you. Merconda, if you could please continue," Dad says with a soft smile.

Acting as if this has been a mere bump in her diatribe, Merconda resumes. “Let us continue.”

For the next hour, we run through every detail, every nuance, and every point that I’d rather forget. But, I have no choice.

Neither does Doll, or Whiskey.

Chapter Sixteen

Circe

Dealing with my history, reminding myself that our accidents make up who we are, I gently touch the scar on my leg. It's my reminder that they were real to me, and they deserve my attempt at being a better person every moment of the day.

Addressing my estranged mother's sudden appearance was not something I expected to deal with in this setting, but I can do it. At that point in my life, I wanted to forget it all. I changed my name, and closed any ties that could connect me to them. She didn't deserve the cut. She was only trying to give me the best of everything.

That girl, the one who always wanted more, who wanted to be the best, was so different from who I am now. My self-imposed exile made me understand material things were just that; things. It made me understand how badly I needed a true connection with someone. Sure, with Wyatt, I have that now. It's been an uphill battle with his condition, for me to understand it and go with the flow, but it's given me back what I gave away willingly.

I've been really short with my mother, acting awful. Arriving on my doorstep, as it were, I was so afraid to talk to her, so I fell back asleep. She said she wanted to be here when I woke up, hoping we could talk more. So far, we've just been sitting silently as Sali changed over a few IV bags, cleared up trash on the side table, and brought me in a light meal. I haven't really touched it, but I have to admit, the Jell-O here is wicked.

"Circe?"

Tucking the blanket down, I scoop up the spoon, along with the bright red Jell-O, and suck back a whack of the luscious treat.

Muffling an answer around the spoon, "Yeah?"

She's squirming in her seat, trying to figure out how to ask what's bothering her. "Where have you been? I mean, I know you left the States for a while, but I didn't know where you ended up. Well, so that this," she says quietly, flourishing her hands in the air, "happened to you."

Nodding a response, I resign myself to the line of questioning I knew would be inevitable. "I ended up on a longer road than I can explain in one sentence. Suffice to say, I was living in Cardiff for a couple years, and I've only just gotten back in the States." Mouthing the spoon, pulling in a couple servings of the red goodness, I scrape the bottom of the now empty cup, wishing there was more. The rest of the food on the tray is indescribable. It might have once been a chicken breast and soft pasta in sauce, but it smells odd, and it's not very appealing.

Laying the empty cup and dirty spoon on the tray, I grab up the glass of water and drink it down, as if it's the last freshwater on earth.

"How are you feeling?" she asks sheepishly. Looking over at her, I worry about what to tell her. She seems nervous and awkward. To tell her that my insides are burning, and that my arm is ice cold would seem petty. Most of all, my heart is broken not knowing what's happened with the others. I don't know how to tell her how badly I've missed everything about her, and that I'm really glad she's here.

"Tight," I tell her. "My chest is very tight. The worst thing, honestly, is the itch in my hand. I can't reach it in this stupid cast."

Smiling, reaches down into her oversized purse and pulls out a metal nail file. I squeal with delight.

"Oh, sweet heaven. You're a genius!" Handing me the petite silver bliss maker, I can almost taste the relief. Taking it in hand, I place it just inside the edge of the cast near my thumb and move it back and forth. It's hard to shift it gently without scratching my skin off, but every time it hits the right spot, it's orgasmic. Until it slips.

"Circe, you look encumbered. Will you let me help you, please?" Trepidation is displayed across her features. She's afraid to offer assistance, or to offend me. Fuck, I feel horrible. Extending my arm out, positioning the open side closer to where she sits, my mother gently appeases my itchy skin.

We haven't seen each other in years, and I'm not sure what's happened in all that time in her life, or in Dad's, and how they've been since I left them behind without a word. Locking the feelings down before I cry inconsolably, because to be totally honest, I want someone to confide in and talk to. Hell, I want to know the truth. But that's not her issue, and pushing it on her won't fix it. Patience is what I need. I need *tons* of patience. The best I can offer her right now is a starting point on repairing our relationship.

"And I thought bringing you a good coffee would be a welcome respite." Poking her head around the curtain, I'm relieved to see my friend.

"Did you happen to find—"

"Psh! Of course I found you a triple mocha, half-caf, nonfat latte. Who would doubt me?" Smiling at my mother, I take in the confusion in Carli's eyes.

Tears threaten to spill out as I take the glorious smelling concoction from her. "I missed you."

Sarcasm lights her features. "Well, who else would know your likes and dislikes, Raggedy Ann?" Pulling over a chair, she reaches a hand out to my mom. "By the way, I'm the best friend, confidant, and all 'round better half to Circe. You must be related."

Carli knows some things about me. Not much, as I kept it pretty locked down, but even an idiot could see the resemblance. "Carli Katana. This is my mother, Natalie Matcheson."

Seeming offended with my introductions, Carli extends her hand across the bed for my mother to shake. "Hard to miss the resemblance." Turning to me with a WTF look, Carli quips off like she does in awkward situations. "I always figured you weren't hatched in an incubator, so someone had to be your mother."

Mouthing to her that I'll explain later, I sip my coffee. Sweet, addictive, and totally required.

"Kubanwan." Turning toward my mother, with a confused look on my face, I listen as she speaks Japanese.

Returning the greeting, Carli bows slightly, grinning from ear to ear.

"You know Japanese?"

"Sukoshi." Winking, she releases Carli's hand and returns to the nail file.

Kicking back on the chair, placing her black pumps on the bed beside my legs, Carli turns. "So, wanna tell me why I can't tell you anything about anything? What's with the lawyering up before I visit?"

"I wish I knew. Mom said she's sworn to secrecy too. It's driving me crazy."

Sipping her green tea—because that's all Carli buys—she blatantly avoids me, just like my mother has.

"Come on. Someone has to tell me something." Now that I'm receiving my caffeine, I'm even more adamant about knowing.

"Sorry, no can do. Strict disclosure confidentiality clauses. The lawyers in the hall, with police—who are sexy as fuck, I might add—are very good at listening in I'm told."

Fuck. I thought for sure Carli would be the one to give up something. Knowing patience with Carli is a necessity, I'll just have to butter up her ass later. "Thanks for the coffee at least, Car."

Sipping it slowly, prolonging the savory treat, I'll wait to see if she'll give me more. The girl cannot keep secrets.

Ever.

I lift my hand away from my mother. "Thanks. That's good." I tuck it back in the bed before the cold from the air conditioning sets in.

"What've you been doing for fun here as you waited for my blazing personality?"

My mother grins, trying to hide the laugh that's forcing its way out. Carli has no idea that she's the entertainment. Always prim and proper, my mother has never been someone who took to someone like Carli. Her friends are direct, crass and richly appointed, always very contained in their conversations. Sarcasm and wit haven't had a place in her lifestyle.

"How about I leave you two alone for a while?" my mother says, gathering her purse and rising out of the chair. "I'll leave the file for you, just in case you need it again. "Hajimemshite." Bowing herself sharply, I'm still in utter shock as Carli returns the greeting.

Waiting until my mother leaves, I smack Car on the arm. "What the fuck was that?"

"Your mother is very polite." Sipping her drink again, I sit in awe of what the hell just happened.

"You're not going to tell me anything, are you?"

I wait. And wait. And wait. "Carli! Tell me something. Please," I plead.

"Sorry, can't." She purses her lips and tightens her jaw. I know there's nothing she'll say. I'm wasting my breath, for now. "But I brought you this."

Pulling up her oversized Louis Vuitton, she produces the LA Times. "I couldn't love you more. Unless you're hiding a mint chip cookie in that bag too."

"Who do you think I am?" Presenting the paper bag, I know she's thought of everything for this visit.

Placing it on the travel table, I open the Times. Flipping through the first few pages, there's only the arts, sports (both butchered), and the entertainment section.

"You know you're a horrible friend, right?"

"It's the best I could get in here. They tore it apart. I'd hid it in my fashion magazine, but I'm betting I'm not the first to attempt it. Sorry, lover, but I can't lose my job with the Gov for smuggling. I had to fight the plain clothes outside the door just for the first few pages of the newspaper." Patting my arm, she tries to soothe my injured soul. "They're hiding it for a reason. I can't help, love."

"You're the second person to say that today."

"Well, at least you know it's not her fault you're clueless." True.

Chapter Seventeen

Wyatt

Another day of watching the nurse, the doctor, various other interns and such perform their duties to keep me alive. I lie still, unmoving and unsettled. I'm not sure I can take much more alone in my own head. Every time I feel this way, the monitors squeak and squeal before attendants rush in, shoving Doll to the side. Every so often, I feel a chill on my body, then hear the monitor's chime. Is this a precursor to another point when everything goes black? I believe so.

Yep. I need to relax. I need to accept that I can't do anything in this state. But fuck, I need to be released from this mental prison. I've yelled, railed, and screamed within these confines, with no movement or flicker of hope for my bludgeoned psyche. The unfortunate silence gives me time to ponder the way our parents slotted us into our new positions. Did I want the position, the responsibility that meant I had to leave the pavement? No. Will I ever have the chance to touch pavement again with rubber? So many questions, so many unanswered revelations as I've contended with my fate.

Will I survive this? Or am I chained, living in servitude to my own memories and fears?

Fuck no. That I won't survive. But how do you escape such a fate when you have no idea how to wake?

Once more, my sister sits in that same uncomfortable chair/pallet that can't be any more comfortable than lying on the floor with pillows and a blanket. Doll talks to me as if I'm able to respond.

"Wake the fuck up, Wyatt. I'm not doing this alone. Don't you dare make me lose another family member. I won't cope." God, Doll, I so wish I could. Believe me, once I'm awake (and I will be), I'll never leave you to deal with anything alone again. *That* I promise you.

Tiring out easily, I feel my body needing rest. Closing my eyes is a silly notion, but resting my worried mind is achievable. So I do.

Chapter Eighteen

Circe

Reliving the accident that changed my life, shaping the person I came to be, makes me yearn for the girls and the life they missed out on.

Once more, the knots in my stomach, like devilish worms, weed their way through my brain like little terrorists. Everything is so hard to accept. It plagues my heart to have no knowledge of him. Dealing with this tight heartache, I'm missing Wyatt terribly. I don't know anything, and it makes my skin itch not having answers.

It's funny. I never found myself finding a guy like him. He reminds me of everything I gave up. The fame, the thrill of an exhilarating sport, the money and the family that was left behind. It's ironic, actually, that I find my life being crushed into a million pieces on the same highway years later.

Every day has been the same, and counting the days is difficult. It consists of more awake hours than sleep now, to the credit of the lovely and talented nurse Sali, and the drop in her drug pushing skills. But being the good patient that I am, I've popped every pill sent my way to avoid the crushing pain in my chest. Dr. Callie has stopped trying to sedate me after I stopped asking about the Crown's.

The annoying, burning itch in my arm is something I can handle, but the pulling and contracting chest muscles that argue every time I breathe makes me feel like a wheezing ex-smoker, or a waitlist lung transplant recipient.

My mother has visited every waking hour, and then some, to make sure I'm doing all right. Carli left me her number on the side table, and even though the phone doesn't have texting abilities I call her incessantly. She left, returning back to Indianapolis on the campaign trail, trying to tie up the Governor's position. That woman is a machine. She even left instructions with my mother on how to get my coffee fix and where, then hit on the sweet police officer that escorted her away. That was just as she was about to finally spill the beans. One of the freakin' nurses overheard our conversation. I swear the room is bugged. That was a few days ago, and it's back to business as usual—me prone on the bed, and my mother bringing in food to keep me nourished.

Really, I don't mind her around all the time, as it's more company than I had previously. Still, it drags me back to the past when she's around. It's a constant reminder of how everything brought me here. And at the same time, it helps me stay sane.

Yes, I'm glad she took that giant leap of faith that I would see her, that I'd accept her visit.

With her out of my life for so long, I wasn't quite sure how to act around her. Was she here looking for the girl who left home in the middle of the night on her eighteenth birthday, with a written note left on the pillow of sorry and thanks? Or was she looking to restart our mother-daughter relationship? Myself, I'm hoping for redemption. Back then, I was only thinking about myself, not about her feelings at all. Now I understand the pain of not knowing how someone you love is fairing without you.

"Is it fine to come back in yet?" she asks from the doorway, peeking her head in.

"Yeah." Pulling the blanket back around my chest one-handed, I grab the water from the table and try to pour a glassful.

"How'd it go?" As the doctor exits, and my mother enters, I answer.

"Good. The doctor said I should be ready to start physio. I have to," I pull in a heavy breath, "start conditioning my lungs to work properly again. I'll have to get my stamina back up so I'm not bedridden." It takes a great deal of work to speak a full sentence without breaks, but I'm excited to get out of bed. To me, it means freedom. Maybe I'll even find out about Wyatt and Marca.

Watching my mother's beaming smile, a smile that's easy and carefree, I'm glad to see her. Meeting her on the street, you'd think she was thirty-something, not almost fifty-something. There's sparsely a gray hair in her sun-kissed, strawberry, sun-highlighted hair. Her green eyes are lit up—a strong, crisp, bright mint behind her long full lashes. Hoping to be as gorgeous as her when I'm her age is something I'll want for sure; she's timeless.

If my path in life hadn't taken me from home, would all of this have happened? Was it destined for us to meet, Wyatt and I? Would my mother and Marca hit it off, I wonder? Would they become fast friends or enemies?

Everything I did changed her life too, and I constantly remind myself of that. Leaving the house with a bag of light clothing and liquid assets, I had no credit cards, no driver's license, and nothing that stated Circe Matcheson. I was reborn on the back of a really good, yet not so reputable source, as Circe Maco. Hopping a plane out of the States, I went to school in Britain, then worked and lived in poverty in Cardiff until my chance encounter with Wyatt. Mom and I have talked at length about it. She explained what happened with her and my dad when I left as they searched for me, using every resource they had, hoping to find me.

Mom and Dad? Well, they didn't last. Her words were that he gave up hope early on. He resigned himself to the fact that I'd decided my family wasn't important. He left her for a younger woman, and now has a new family in Texas.

"Time for your meds," Sali says as she enters the room in a breeze, toting behind her the bloodwork cart.

Shifting the bed up a bit, I prepare myself for her devilish ways. "Oh goodie, the vampire is back." Smirking, I lay my arm on the bed for her ministrations as she gathers up the necessary accessories.

"Well, it's a painful job, but someone has to torture patients on a daily basis."

"I'm glad those dominatrix online courses came in handy," I tell her. She laughs, drawing blood into the vials before slipping me a water glass, and the tiny cup with various little pills.

Handing the empty cup back to her, she tosses it in the trash. "How are you today? Is your chest sore?" Sali chirps, taking my pulse and blood pressure.

"Better," I say on a tight breath.

"Good. Hopefully, we can get you up in a wheelchair tomorrow so you can—"

"Tomorrow! I can get out of this nine-by-nine prison? Sweet." The joy must be written across my face, even though I'm wheezing as I speak. She grins in return and honestly, I can't wait.

"For now, though, I need you to get more sleep." Looking to my mom, she nods her acceptance. Rising from the chair, she follows my nurse and her evil cart out. I'm alone, and really tired.

As she exits, she says to me, "Have a good sleep, sweetheart."

"Thanks." Watching her leave, Sali closes the door behind them.

"Fine. I can do this." I express my excitement to the vacant room. "Tomorrow I'm blowing this pop-shop to find me something sexy. Wyatt, be ready. I'm coming to get your ass." I know my grin must be a mile wide, but I'm excited for what's to come.

Pushing the button, reclining the bed, I look forward to the opportunity to see Wyatt for myself. If I have to, I'll search the whole damn hospital until I find either, a corpse, or his prone soul on a bed like mine.

Waiting will be torturous.

That night, my dreams have me reliving everything from the first moment to the last, but I always return to that first night we met. It was crazy. It was awesome. All of it brought me to him.

To us.

Chapter Nineteen

Wyatt

Being in this state, I remember being with Circe. Then a time when she wasn't in my life, when Dad was still here. Being at the house and enjoying every moment with my father before a race, my mind reenacts it all. Then he's gone, and I'm alone.

I've dealt with sadness, with being scared, and the confusion of my own volatile mind as I wade through it all. I'm thinking and overthinking things.

Yes, I'm still trapped in this stinking hospital room, watching my sister like a specter as she sleeps uncomfortably in the chair, hardly resting. There's times I listen in as she speaks with the doctor about my care. More and more, I feel disgusted that she's been thrust into this. At times, my brother and sister talk in hushed tones about the house, mother, my care. Or oddly enough, there's silly moments when they think about days that were simpler. I listen as they rehash old wounds, think on the happier times, and even converse as a brother and sister should.

The danger of being trapped here; I don't know how long I can handle my own thoughts as company. The pressure of only me, myself, and the other fella that likes to fall into a deep abyss of despair and desolation is a battle I may not win.

Crying out for mental freedom, I'm a tortured hostage as I'm thrust back into the present. Anger is a necessary evil flooding me in these moments. I think about all that I'm missing out on. I have an overwhelming explosion of happiness as I think of Circe. Then, an unwavering sadness that hangs like a pall over my head. Everything is a regret. I was never able to be the man my father wanted me to be. I don't have it in me. I know that with certainty.

FUCK!

I hate being stuck.

I *want* to be with her.

Siren.

Regretting that I'm not more worried about my mother and her outcome is a pain I'll deal with later. Right now, I need *her*. Knowing if she's safe is a driving need.

With nothing else to do, I watch Doll. Taking stock of the strong woman she's become, I'm proud of her. She holds her ground with Whiskey. Watching their interactions, the two of them have a heated argument in the hall. As usual, she's stronger than he gave her credit for. Don't ask how I see everything, yet can't react. It doesn't make sense, but I do. She seems utterly pissed off about something, and Whiskey, in his usual aloof attitude, is blowing off her serious conversation. Giving in or giving up, Doll leaves as Whiskey wanders in.

Slamming the door, he positions himself in the chair with a huff. I expect him to be silent and despondent as usual, but surprising me, he speaks. "Fuck, Cas. Hurry the hell up. The last thing I want to do is deal with the bullshit you're intended for." Pulling out his phone, scrolling through emails or posts, everything about our world crashes around us. I wish so badly to answer him.

Absently talking for the sake of chatting, Jamieson stuffs his phone back in his pocket and continues. "Remember that ramp we built? Fuck. I thought mom was going to kill us both."

Memory lane with him? Huh. Okay, I can do this.

Listening to his deep breathing as he thinks about the past, it's melodic and relaxing. "We were racing. You rode that bike of mine down, crashed into the side of Dad's Bentley, and I slid down my side on a board, straight into the garage. I took out a stack of plants Ciccero was repotting. Man, we got our asses handed to us. I thought for sure Mom would have coronary on the spot." He pauses. I bet he's thinking the same as me. "Well, I guess it doesn't matter anymore. That's something I can't fix."

Clearing his throat, he rises out of the chair, as if it's made of brimstone and fire. He heads for the door as Doll reenters with two coffees in hand.

"Where are you going, Whiskey?"

"Something came up." Grabbing the outstretched cup, he opens the door open. "I'll grab you lunch if you want. Text me later."

And there's the consummate brother I know. He's always ran from family obligations. No, it's true he wasn't meant for this, but he'd better damn well be looking after Doll. Once I'm up, if he isn't, I'll kick his ass.

Our family business never had any sway over Jamieson. No pull at all. He never affiliated himself with the Crown Industries label, and it's because Mom and Dad created this strife.

We used to love each other. Sure, our lives were all different because of age, but we always cared. It was the common link. Remembering a time when we were all together, in the same house, dealing with family drama and politics as children, my mind sways...

The party is in full swing. Even though there's a mansion full of teenagers and sponsors milling around, Doll wants me to take her outside to our track. Bad freakin' idea I said, but she'll do it either way. It's bad enough I have an obsession with speed and danger, at least that's what Mother tells me consistently. She's somewhat resigned to it now, knowing there's no stopping me. That minuscule chance that I could die in her backyard scares the living hell out of her. It frightens her to no avail. Now there's no trying to drag Doll away from it either. It's in our blood, in our genes. It's a calling. Danger is an aphrodisiac like no other.

Mother, though, wants her children playing safe sports. Things like tennis, water polo, badminton, or lawn bowling. Floor hockey, soccer, and racing aren't sports to her. They're too dangerous to be considered a sport. They're barbaric, requiring padding, controlled environments, doctors and surgeons on call.

But that's all we know. The chance that you could be hurt, maimed, or killed in a second because of a jellybean on the track, that's what she wants to save her children from. She wants what every mother wants. She wants us to outlive her and our father, but that tender, motherly side is never shown. When she wants us to quit, it's in shouts, screaming fits, and manic moments that include pieces of porcelain embedded into the walls.

"Come on. Let's go, Cas!" Doll's squeaky little girl voice peels over the den of the room, gathering the attention of those close. It always has, it always will. Doll has a way of engaging the masses to her every command. My little sister has a way with people, where they feel obligated to love, listen, and above all, cherish her. She obviously has me and Dad at her beck and call. Whiskey, not so much. Mom sees through her sweetness.

"Cas, you coming? I really want to try it out. I want you there for the first time."

"Yeah, Doll." There she is, standing by the open doors of the living room with an outfit on that if Mother could see it right now, it would send her into a coma. She's very busy with this event, thank fuck. At this point, she hasn't noticed her, yet.

Doll's long legs are encased in black riding pants. Wearing a bright pink, full armor jacket, she saunters across the steps, holding her demonic painted helmet. It dangles helplessly from her petite fingers that are better suited to piano keys than holding a throttle. But who am I to judge?

Mother has tried time and again to get her to complete her lessons, finish her latest concerto, or prepare for her next ballet recital. Good luck. Unfortunately, Mother, all your children take after their father, and less after the ballet princesses and chess matchmakers of the world than you can mentally handle. There's no holding Doll back when she decides she's doing something, and if Mom can't handle it, she's just going to have to get over it with a blindfold and Percocet's.

Strutting across the expansive room, the way I always do, it's what my mom calls a swagger. "Yeah, I'm here, Doll," I mutter, "Like I'd rather be inside?" I say to myself as I look back at the full house. I'd do anything to avoid the soiree.

Taking off for the track, slinging her long chocolate hair behind her, Doll flings the helmet on. She looks ready to take on the world. The sinister designs on her helmet virtually moves as she bounds across the yard.

Picking up the pace to match her fast walk, I catch up. Doll will go off on her own without a thought to safety on her brand-new ride. She won't care what it looks like with a party full of investors and sponsors if she crashes, or if she takes a turn too wildly. A spill could kill her chances of ever becoming a sponsored pro. I know it's what fuels her, and I know it's useless to stop her. Hell, it was useless to stop me.

As I almost catch my sister, I hear my name shouted across the porch. "Wyatt."

Fuck.

Stopping dead in my tracks and look up. Her stature looks poised, yet deadly as she leans on the stone railing. I walk back over.

"Yes, Mother?"

"Darling," she says sugar sweet through tight lips. "Please keep your sister off the track while I entertain." Raising her skimpy index finger, she wiggles it for me to follow. Smiling tightly, that sarcastic 'I'm holding my shit together, Wyatt' look crests her features. She's pissed. Not that it's hard to tell. The stiff walk, the hard step, and the air of 'fuck off' is thick.

With a haughty huff escaping her, she crosses her arms, pointing to Doll.

"This, Wyatt," she points to Doll, "is utterly embarrassing. These parties are for you, your sister—"

"And Whiskey," I interject.

Ignoring my outburst, hardly showing any reaction, other than a tightening of her gaze, she continues. "And, of course, this is for your father. We want your racing to be successful. Please keep her off the track. I expressly expect you to have this under control, quickly."

"When did I become her—"

"Yes, Wyatt," she snaps. "You are her jailer today, yesterday, and every day." She walks away, knowing the conversation is complete in her mind. "Control her," she states harshly over her shoulder, returning to her guests. Her decision is made. Either I'll look after Doll, or she'll make my life a living nightmare.

Fuck.

My mother has a way that riles me up. We fight, someone ends up sedated, and normally, I fall into a fog of drugs. Today, I don't need to be put down, therefore I guess I gained the position of sitter for hire. Passing out the door, away from the festivities, I walk as fast I can to catch up again. Taking the steps two at a time, I race down. Neither of us need the bullshit later.

"Doll, wait up, will ya!" I yell ahead, hoping she'll stop. Miraculously, she does.

With her hands on her hips, arms indignantly stiff, her head sags forward in that motion that tells me she's pissed. Great, both of them annoyed at me. This is the last thing I need today.

Knowing how to turn every last wheel in my head, making me feel bad for arresting her fun, Doll pipes up angrily. "What, Cas? You gonna tell me that it's not a good time?" Peering at me through the visor with those crystal green eyes, they pierce into your soul and make you pliable, and giving. Every. Single. Time.

Smiling, I cock my head to the side, giving her the same look back. We both have a way of making people do our bidding, she just has a better grasp on how to twist her brother into knots.

"I was just going to say it's—"

"No, I'm not backing down, Casper. I want to try the track. My bike is fine, the day is fine, the outfit is perfectly formed. Mom's inside, hosting a slew of indignant pompous a-holes, and I want to enjoy the day." She crosses her arms across her chest, trying to scowl. Letting out that haughty preteen huff once more, she knows I'm the one person she can't win with if I decide it's best for both of us.

"Look. Later, I'll grab mine and we'll go out." I level a look on her that brokers no room for argument. "But it will be on my terms, Doll. Now stop being a spoiled rich kid and go hang with the others." It's not like I'm lying. I had every intention to go on the track after the party anyway.

"Give me your helmet." Dragging the helmet over her head, shaking out her hair, she hands it to me. I smirk.

"You better be willing to get your ass kicked in a few hours, because that's all I'm giving you."

"Good luck, Doll. Big brother's gonna kick your ass again." I call after her, grinning like the crazy fool I am. Falling directly into her snare, hook, line, and sinker, she won. Flipping me the bird over her shoulder, she hops up the back stairs.

What I wouldn't have done to avoid the bullshit inside, just like her? Hitting the track with her is more pleasurable than any crap going on in the house.

Walking the remainder of the way across the yard to the drive shed, I punch in the code and step inside. Flicking a switch, the room lights up, showcasing all of its glory. It houses two of my dad's cars, three extra bays for working on new acquisitions, and enough space for both our bikes. And when I say bikes, I mean the scraps leftover from numerous errors on turns. It's a fucking graveyard in here.

Passing by the latest victim of family road kisses, Dad's car looks like it took on a Mack truck and lost. Truth isn't far off the mark. The walls are unforgiving bastards, and even less sympathetic are the drivers that pass you by. Oh, of course they feel bad you're out, or hurt. Though once the bling is on their finger and the cup's in their hands, all bets are off. That is, until the next lap or race day.

Remorse and regret are horrible companions on the track.

Stepping around the heap of metal, clambering over shards of a fairing, a quarter fender, and a discombobulated hood scoop, I place her helmet lovingly on the rack beside mine. The bright overhead lights lay shadows across the tanks of our bikes, showing every small blemish and scratch from bad practice runs or scuff-ups with another rider. The love I have for this sport means I can't see myself ever leaving it. The passion and exhilaration go hand in hand. Without it, I think I'd curl up in a ball and never feel the touch of greatness again. That's the danger of living in my head, shit is wrapped up in remorse, regrets, dangerous comments of "you're not good enough," or the sad conviction of being the disappointment to my dear Mother.

Clearing the depression from my thoughts, I pat the top of my helmet lovingly. It's my third arm if you will. My helmet is the part that I can't be without. It's plain, no distinguishing marks, no bright colors, and no designs. Just a plain flat black. Doll's, on the other hand, is a tapestry in comparison. The brilliant pink leaves, the surreal skulls and purple roses on her helmet look haunting and ethereal. Like I said, it totally marks who she is. She's a dangerous China Doll, one that can cut your heart out with a spoon if given a chance. The girl inside that helmet is not a natural being. She is fearless, and nasty. Even though she looks like a princess, she'd rather take your head off with a scythe if you even dare try to cut her off on the track. Nastiest twelve-year-old on the track for sure.

Leaving and walking back out to the bright light of day, resigning myself to the fact that there's no way out of it, I lock up the garage. I head back to the house, and the party that I don't intend on participating in further. Again, my name is called.

"Wyatt?"

Fuck.

"What's wrong, Mother?"

She glares at me, that same look. "Don't be sardonic with me. If you didn't have that track, both of you—"

"Yeah," I cut her off. "We'd be inside shaking hands, smiling, and drumming up sponsors for the Crown team."

She squints at me and I swear, if she was a cartoon character, I'd see flames erupting out of her eyes. She's trying her best to fry me in my expensive Armani loafers, as I'm doing my best to keep my cool.

"I'm truly disappointed in you. Please keep yourself inside, smiling and sweet for the remainder of the day. I fully expected more of you." Without an opportunity to answer her, she turns on her heels and heads back into the foray of big wallets wanting to say they're a part of Crown Racing's winning ride. Dad will be in there somewhere, doing his part. As his adoring children, Mother expects the same of us. We are expected to be doting, entertaining, and the perfect hosts.

What bullshit.

With a few fake smiles to a few of the bigger sponsors, I head to my room. There I can be alone. I can be with others if need be, and I can avoid an all-out war with Marca Crown.

Passing Whiskey's room, the music is blaring, something dark and emo as usual. Knowing him, he's regretting the summer break at home with family. We don't see him much anymore with his race team, his sponsorship runs, and the overall schmooze fests in ski country. Knocking, I wait for his reply. We're only five years apart in age, but we might as well be complete strangers for how much we know of each other.

Opening the door, his gargantuan form blocks the doorway. Built like Dad, and a temper like a raging bull, we haven't really spoke since he got home.

"Hey. What's up?" His brisk demeanor is actually almost sweet.

"Just figured if you weren't doing anything, we could go to the gym and spar for a bit. I need to toss off some tension. Thought maybe you could do with it too."

"Yeah, sounds good." Nodding, he turns off his stereo and snatches up a pair of runners. We bound gleefully down to the first floor to work off family tension.

Chapter Twenty

China

Before Dad's death, I never understood loss. Not real loss.

Not this.

This is *epic* shit.

Weeks have passed—fucking years if you asked me—and the last thing I want to be doing is sitting *here*, waiting in the chapel of the hospital. I'm the first to arrive before Whiskey, the chaplain, and our parents' lawyers. They said they'd control all the needs that had to do with Mom, Wyatt, Circe's care, the 'razzi' and all the bullshit that a *young woman* shouldn't have to handle. If I really wanted to deal with these things, I'd rail at them to stop treating me like a fucking ten-year-old. As it is, I want to be left alone to deal on my own, to handle the grief. To wait for Wyatt.

My emotions are jacked and I'm holding my shit together by a thin wire as best I can. My heart can't take much more, and I'm not sure I'll ever be able to put myself back together if Wyatt...I can't even find myself saying it internally.

I won't.

I can't imagine my brother gone from my life. He's my confidante, my shoulder to punch, my race partner, the guy who keeps the bad blood at bay when I'm treated as a nuisance in my own home, and the one who's kept me laughing through it all, even when all he wanted to do was cry and curl up in a ball himself. Honestly, I think part of the reason he's taking so long to wake from the coma is that his head knows it needs time to process everything that's happened. Over the years, he's dealt with being a bipolar manic depressive. It's had an iron grip on his soul. It was the one thing bringing him down, hardening him to human connection. I knew that. I knew that it was always hard for him to deal with others. And how he hid it so well, for so long? I knew the track was his main release, outside of women. Only his closest friends are privileged enough to know what he contends with. They'd seen how

Mother could send him into a rage, into a depressive state, and how she created it all. For sure, I'm glad that I don't deal with the same demons they do, or did. My only demon is my bike and how I ride it.

"Doll?"

Turning, I see Whiskey standing in the half-lit entrance. Looking at him, his stature, his frame, his mannerisms and poise, all I see is Dad. He knows how much he looks like him, and even though we haven't lived together since I was little, I can see the heartache as it creeps across his stern features.

Fuck, I miss Dad.

"Hey," I say, rising from the pew, waiting for him to come to me.

We've never had a relationship. With too many years between us, and a country that's divided us, it's never been feasible. He left when he was sixteen to live out west with Auntie Janie. I was only six. The little brat that would chase him around the house pestering him, cramping his teenage lifestyle. That was me.

It's funny, really, in the past two months with Dad, this with Mom, Wyatt, and Circe, I've seen him more now than I ever did back then. It hasn't made our relationship better, just more current.

"Hey. Any news?" he asks. His raspy voice is deep, scratchy, and not unlike Wyatt's. It makes me wistful. Shaking the feeling of sadness, grounding myself in the knowledge that he's still here, he's still with me, but sleeping like a lazy fucker, I smile weakly.

"No, not yet." Whiskey had a championship to attend just before coming here. He was in the middle of his races and not expected until the next day originally, but when he heard about the crash, a few flights later, he was here. That was over a month ago.

"What were you doing? I thought you were just heading to the house for a bit?"

"Crown Industries booked a meeting with the press. I was commanded to be there by Merconda," he states, sauntering up the aisle toward me. "Have you been waiting long?"

"No." I motion to the wooden bench. As he sits, I take another seat.

It's hard when you have nothing to talk about, except for morbid conversation. What do you talk about? We're not engaging each other for the sake of talking. We don't want to break the silence with a stupid comment. Instead, we're taking in each other's melancholic presence. We haven't really *talked* talked either. Yeah, I called him, gave him the rundown about the crash, and he's been here off and on. But we're disconnected. He's ran around for me, grabbing things and dealing with shit. It hasn't been easy on either of us. We've argued a few times, but nothing important was talked about. Both of us are avoiding the elephant in the room. Honestly, it all sucks fucking balls.

"Sorry," he says with sincerity. Taking my hand in his, I look into his face. I see the same care and love reflected back. He's a mirror image of Dad. It's crushing.

"James, this is great, really. Thank you for being here." I've done everything I can to hold it in. Keeping my shit together in public and around the staff, but the weight of it is crushing me. I just can't hold it back anymore.

As the floodgates open, I fall apart. Tears stream down my face in a torrent of rain. Everything around me falls into despair as I lay my head in the crook of his arm. Gasping between coughing breaths, I feel his hand on my head, stroking me, making the feeling of loneliness even more apparent. He's been gone for so long that we're like cousins. We aren't sister, brother, mother and father to him, and they made this happen, creating less family along the way.

"Let it go, China. It'll be okay...somehow." I hear him choking back a tear or two of his own, but the sound is drowned out by my total heartbreak. It annihilates me, taking over. I've held it in for so long that I'm not sure how I'll put myself back together after letting it go. He may be here to take part of the burden away, but it still feels so shattering.

In my despair, I don't notice the door of the chapel as it opens, nor do I hear the chaplain as I collapse into hopelessness.

"It's okay. Hang on, China. I've got you." Hearing Jamieson's voice so closely resembling Dad's and Wyatt's, I feel a renewed wave of tears tumble down. I'm sobbing uncontrollably.

Vaguely, I adjust as the lights of the chapel brighten. Hearing the scratching of shoes across the floor and the words of Whiskey as he tries to calm me down, I try not to pass out.

Chapter Twenty-One

Circe

I miss him so much, Mom." I'm sobbing uncontrollably and it hurts every fiber in my body. It's been weeks with no word.

She pets my back, soothing me, calming me as I shake. "It'll be okay, Circe. It'll be okay."

I've completely and utterly had enough of these consistent weeks of no info on his status. No one is telling me if he lived or died. Do I need to deal with his death? No. It's not real. I won't believe it. My mind still reels, thinking it's a possibility.

It's unbearable, this heartache. The pain is excruciating, and I can't continue this way for much longer. I'm curling in on myself, turning in like Wyatt has in the past. I know how it is to see it, feel it, and be a part of it. Now I'm living it.

"Circe, honey. It's going to be fine. Just breathe for me, sweetheart." I hear my mom say, just as Sali arrives. Shuffling around, pulling on the IV tube that's connected to my hand, she plunges something in.

"Time to sleep, Circe," I hear her say. The effect is fast.

As I drift off, I hear my mother and Sali speaking. "She's not dealing with this, Sali."

"I'll try to do something more. But I can only do so much, Natalie."

"I understand. Do what you can."

Chapter Twenty-Two

China

Now I understand the saying, *shit rolls downhill.*

As my emotional dam bursts, I let the tears flow freely and fast. Whiskey appearing in that chapel was like an apparition. Dad was standing there, caring for me, watching over me inside the fog of my mind as I fell apart. That was days ago, and now I'm back to my usual hold-it-in self.

Whiskey had me sedated for the rest of the day as he watched over Cas. Thank fuck. I needed it, I guess. I needed to let go and let everything take over; at least that's what Dr. Callie said. To top it off? Over the past week, Wyatt's body has decided to shut down a few more times to give me a mental freakin' breakdown.

Thanks, Wyatt.

Like I can take any more pressure, asshole. Those bloody monitors go off, lighting up like Christmas trees in Times Square, causing every doctor, nurse, and sidekick to show up. His heart has stopped twice, and it's making me crazy. I think I'm about to lose my ever-loving shit.

Yesterday, it was calm and peaceful, running up to that ticker quitting again. We thought he was dreaming. He must have had a nightmare, throwing him into a panic attack of sorts, tossing him into an irregular heart rate. It was boom! Defib and paddles. Sleeping was not sleeping after all, brother. Minutes later, he was back, and I began breathing. Now I stay awake all hours of the day, just so I can keep track of my big brother.

Since our moment in the chapel, Jamieson has come by a lot more. He brought me by a jump bag this morning. He took me to lunch as Sali watched Wyatt, but we didn't talk much. He never hangs around long, and whenever it's a point I think we could have a heart to heart, he's gone. Something is going on, but I don't know what it is. It's a secret. Whiskey is a secret type of guy, which means little China Doll is expected to keep the peace, smile nicely, and be sweet to Whiskey.

He avoids both of us like we're a burden, or like a date with the gynecologist.

It's crazy. I mean, Wyatt is the one here on the bed. Mom is...well, let's not get into that. Dad is dead, and I'm alone. My biggest worry right now is me. I'm trying to keep my control together, so I don't have a complete breakdown. It won't help Wyatt any if I'm laid up in a loony bin.

Since this began, I've completely and unequivocally avoided anything that has to do with Mom, Dad, and Circe. Don't get me wrong, I know Wyatt would kick my ass if he thought I wasn't caring for her, so I am, but I just can't handle giving her updates every day on his non-progression. So I told the Doc and Sali to keep her in the dark about Wyatt's condition. I've asked them to keep me abreast of her needs, and I made sure her medical bills were being cared for by Crown. Jamieson didn't like it at first, but I was adamant. I'm doing that whether he likes it or not. She may not be a Crown, but she's important to Wyatt, and that's what counts.

Fuck!

When will shit stop?

I'm sick of it falling in my lap.

What I wouldn't give to be on my bike, riding the blacktop and scraping my knees on the corners. Maybe I'll get Whiskey to ride my street bike over. I've been the one on lockdown in this sterile jail, and *I* need a moment out for good behavior. I'm itching to touch the pavement. A release of endorphins will help with the tears. I'll push them right out at a hundred and ninety miles an hour.

My girlfriends still pop over, but they have to go through so much security, you'd think they were visiting the fucking Pope. Whiskey sucks at sticking around and making me feel better about the whole situation, which I understand. Honestly, he hasn't lived with the family...

Fuck, now there's a joke—family. That's gone. Like poof, missing, disappear-o, finito. I sit here, hoping for Casper to wake up, to tell me everything will be fine, and it was all a bad dream. But our family will never be whole. It's gone. Now it's just us.

"All I need is a sign, Wyatt. Just one word." I'm feeling so alone that I talk to him like he can hear me. Screw that. I'm not alone. That's the wrong analogy. I'm fucking separated on an undiscovered island, filled with coconut trees and ugly fucking monkeys, *alone.*

I've read every magazine, watched all the soap operas I can handle, and even flicked to some of the who's your daddy shows just to bypass the despair. It works about as well as dousing my heart in arsenic. The real shit part is, I can't really leave this place either. I'm chained to his bed until he wakes up. *If.*

Dammit. Do I have to find another goddamn casket? I've had enough of caskets, urns, and bullshit. My twenty-first birthday was supposed to be a celebration. In mere weeks, I'm an adult in all the ways that matter. I wasn't looking for new responsibilities and cares. Getting out on my own, away from Mom and Dad, now feels selfish and horrid. Desperately, I wish it were different.

At least Dad would have told me "*Doll, everything works out.*"

Not this time, Dad. You didn't work out, and Mom is a reminder that I have something else to deal with. She's on ice, literally, and until we figure out what's going on with my brother, she'll stay that way.

Showing up around an hour ago Jamieson, as usual, was off like a shot. Excuses are all he needs to vacate this place.

Before leaving, I asked him to bring back my ride. Thankfully, he said he'd have it over this afternoon, so maybe I'll try to run out later while he hangs with Wyatt. At least *he* understands being on lockdown. Sitting in Cali, where there's no snow, he has to be having a meltdown. I haven't hit the track in weeks, and I'm itching for a release. I can just imagine a guy who's used to the cold, sitting still in ninety-eight degree weather. It must be excruciating.

I've also exhausted my three best friends. If it isn't Cathryne popping over with food, it's Harlow, trying to catch a sidelong glance at Whiskey. She's always had a thing for him. I've ran them ragged, having them bring in Starbucks. It's a necessity. The coffee here isn't something I'd put in my engine, never mind my stomach. And don't even get me started on what they consider edible. When Wyatt wakes, he's going to be hungry as a dog and looking for nourishment, of which he won't find here. The food, or what they try to pass off as food, is rubbery chicken, overcooked rice, baked unknown pastas, and wilted salads.

The take-out boys have brought me sushi from Kato's, carbonara from Tulio's, and stuffed salmon from Polar Bear twice this week alone. Feeling bad they have to traverse the overstuffed officers, paparazzi, and professional reporters, just to bring it to me, I've decided they're pretty damn brave. They leave here wilted and concerned they'll be arrested. Crown gave direct instructions to keep everyone out, except those with signed waivers. There's no one to tell me not to spend, not to be extravagant, and no one to tell me to go to school.

Bed.

Don't date.

Don't this, don't that.

No China, can't China.

I'd rather you not, China.

Argh!

"Miss Crown?" Turning toward the partially open door, Sali, Wyatt's daytime nurse, enters. Because of the circumstances surrounding the crash, the popularity of the family, the team, and Wyatt directly, the hospital setup specific nurses and doctor's so that comings and goings could be monitored.

"Hey, Sali." I stretch out a bit in the Barcalounger. Pulling the light covers around my shoulders, I tuck my feet in to keep warm.

"How are things today?" she asks, looking over the monitors, the lines, the incisions, and under the bandage at his head.

He still looks like shit. I won't be the one to tell him that, but he does.

I've seen worse damage from accidents on the track, but none have scared the living hell out of me like this has. The bandage on his head is covering the ten-inch scar that will run along the side of his head. It'll be hidden under his hair when it grows back, thankfully. The swelling has gone down since last week, but there's still no changes in his condition. Dr. Callie has decided to keep him in a drug-induced sleep for a while longer. I hope to hell that the brother I know comes out on the other side of this. Or, if he is changed, then he's controlled.

"Well, I'm still bored stiff and looking for something to pass the time. How are things out there?" I motion toward the front of the building, where I know the masses are still gathered, awaiting news on the Crown family's condition.

"Same," she says.

"I figured as much."

Sali clicks the foot pedals on the mobile bed, turning to me with a smile. "Dr. Callie requested a new MRI and CAT scan today. We're look for changes. Do you want to come along?"

I've gone with Wyatt on these in the past, but for some reason, I don't want to today.

"No. I'll wait here, if that's okay? How long will you be gone?"

Attaching the IV pole and the monitor systems to the gurney, Sali opens the door to the hallway. "I don't think there's anyone else there waiting, so we should be back in about an hour or so. Why don't you go get a shower and something to eat?"

"Thanks. I just might." I can't stand the showers here. There's no pressure, and the food, as I've already stated, is something I wouldn't hand to the homeless.

Being as civil as I can, I smile, rising from the chair. Hopefully, Dr. Callie will see something that will show progress, because I need my brother back.

Chapter Twenty-Three

Circe

Two days ago, I fell apart. I'd had enough. After weeks of being here, I still no nothing about Wyatt and Marca. My waking mind and every thought are damaged. What if I hadn't switched seats? What if my phobia of the back had saved her?

Nurse Sali, my mother, and Dr. Callie tell me it's not healthy to worry about the past, about what I can't do anything about. I shouldn't worry about failures and unfixable situations.

Today is about fixable situations. I'm getting out of this bed, this room, and trying my first day of physio. If I thought it was hard to breathe lying down, sitting upright in a wheelchair has been goddamn near impossible. The pressure is difficult. It's like laying a ten-ton weight across my breastbone.

Excited to get up and about as soon as I was given the go ahead by Dr. Callie, my mother helped my ass into the unloving stiff beast. Venturing out of my room on our floor, we passed a commissary, two nurses stations, a treatment room in the cancer wing, and a chapel. There were a ton of police and professionally dressed men. None of them gave us a moment's notice.

When I was a kid, my parents were religious to a fault, so of course when we passed the chapel, she asked if I felt the need to give thanks. Truly, I'm not sure if I'm thankful after everything that's occurred, or if I feel like railing at an unforgiving being that has caused me so much heartache. For now, I told her that I wished to bypass it.

My high hopes that I would see Whiskey, or Wyatt's sister China in the halls was excessive, as we didn't see anyone I knew. Making me mourn a bit more, the trip down the hall felt wasted. The pain I was suffering was worthless.

Most days, my mother visits early. Now that I'm allowed out, she's taken me on rides through the *castle*, then left just after I passed out in the afternoon. I'm starting to look forward to our talks too. We're catching up, learning who we are as adults, not as mother and daughter. It's funny. There are some things we now have in common that before were polar opposites.

She has a love affair with sappy love stories and raunchy sex novels. We both hate broccoli. We believe that espresso is a necessary evil, and that even though I didn't own a single pair, I still have a penchant for shiny, expensive shoes. One day, she actually brought over a pair of my shoes I left behind, and it reminded me that I was truly a troll when I headed out of there without a word. Funniest part is that the shoes still fit. I grew up, but didn't grow out.

It's been another week of the same routine, and today, I'm at another physio session with Crane, my therapist. Learning how to do things with my right hand has been a blunder. I've been told it'll be at least three more weeks before they remove the cast to put on a soft one. It totally sucks moose balls.

"Try again, Circe," Crane says as I'm learning to lift a pencil in my opposite hand. It's awkward as fuck.

"Good." He's happy with my progress. Dis-appointed in myself, I shouldn't feel like a helpless toddler.

Turning the pencil, I lean into it, looping letters the size of a baseball across the page. It's worse than a kindergartener.

"Do you praise everyone? Or did you just decide to be kind today, Crane?"

"No. I only praise when someone does something right. It's true, you suck. But at least you're trying. That's good."

"I'll keep trying, Mr. Happy."

"Did you work on the breathing exercises I gave you too?" Showing him my progression, as I huff and wheeze like a smoker, it feels like I'm trying to work out at a Lamaze class, but I do as I'm told.

"Okay, you're done for today. Return to your jail, madam." He smirks, man giggles, then pushes my chair toward the door where my mother is. She's looking at her phone, and I know damn well she's looking through the Tinder account that I setup for her. She places the phone in her pocket, stands, then smiles at me.

"Better today?" she asks Crane, twinkling like a teenager. He's cute for an older guy, but she stares at him like he's the best man candy on the planet. He's taller, around six-six, with black and white tattoos covering both arms, a neatly trimmed moustache and beard, and a loosely slicked back, peppered haircut.

"Yes. She was, Natalie." Crane makes it sound sexy. It still makes me laugh to hear my mother addressed by her first name, instead of 'mom'. He watches her intently for a moment or two, then he winks, causing her to blush. Loving that the heat rises in her features, he stares her down like prey, It's nice, actually.

Spinning in my chair, I try to avoid the awkward silence and blatant sexual friction that's flowing between them. "Ready, Mother?"

With a quick nod, she wheels me out to the hall, toward the room. Slamming straight into the oversized elephant, I ask, "Sooo?"

"Nothing, Circe. Crane is just—"

"Yummy?"

"Yes, he's yummy, but not something I need in my life right now. My priority is you." That's a *bow chicka wow wow* moment. I mean, my mom just called someone yummy. It's funny as hell. Admitting that she found him sexy as all get, and that she's avoiding it like the plague to care for me is bogus.

"So, when I'm out of physio, out of the hospital, well and repaired, will you then take a shot at Crane?"

She thinks about it for a second. I can physically see the wheels spinning as she considers her words wisely.

"No."

"No?"

"No, Circe. I'll think about a man when it's time for me to, not when the time accommodates your schedule."

"Fine," I laugh, "I'll leave you alone about—" Pausing mid-sentence, my heart stops. Seeing someone I never expected to see, my mother frets over my sharp intake of air.

"Are you okay, Circe?"

Standing casually beside the nurse's station is one person I'd know anywhere, and excited to see. "China?"

Freezing in place, she slowly looks over her shoulder at me, like a scared rabbit. "Hi, Circe."

Nervous, giddy, and unsure, I blurt out. "Are you here to see me?" The first time I might have a chance at answers, and she's standing right there.

"No, sorry. I'm just talking to the day nurse to see if I can grab a few more blankets. Some moron turned up the a/c in our room. I figure if I'm freezing—" catching herself saying something she doesn't want to, she stops. Her mouth is set harshly as she tries to hold in her words.

Knowing she's hiding something from me, I break the pregnant pause. "China. Is it Wyatt? Is Wyatt, okay?"

China's shock is visible. She didn't expect me to push her further. Taking in the my old man cart she smiles. Genuine and sincere, China steps forward with her hand outstretched. "*And* you are?"

"Natalie Matcheson. Circe's mother."

"Even though I've never heard about you, it's nice to meet you." Wow. Nasty, cutting, and sweet as she avoids.

"It's nice to meet you too, China. Over the past few days, Circe has told me quite a bit about you and your family."

Seeing China's face drop, it shows fear, sadness, despair, doubt, anger, rage and sympathy. Schooling her face to look calm and composed, China smiles tightly. "I'm sorry, but I need to get these blankets back to the room." Spinning on her heels as fast as possible, China starts down the opposite hall from us, off to where I assume Wyatt and Marca are guarded. I feel horrible, but I have to push it. I need to know.

"China, please. *Please* tell me." I plead.

Stopping, then turning back, her face is set in a hard line. "I'm sorry," Is all she says moving away without another word.

"China! Please," I yell, "Please. Tell me something!"

Tears choke me, pain surrounds me, and the need to jump from this prison like chair is all I can think of. Attempting to rise, my mom gently presses her hands into my shoulders, holding me in place. "Circe, no. Let her go."

Resigning, dragging in a deep breath, I hold in the emotions attempting to flood forth. "Can we go back to the room? I'm tired all of a sudden."

"Sure."

Chapter Twenty-Four

Circe

D

amaged souls, how may I direct you call?" Witty. For once, it doesn't make me smile.

"I saw China today."

The line is quiet, with only her breath to be heard. "Fuck."

I don't have the space in my heart to react yet.

"Car, give me something, please."

"Love, I wish I could, really. The Governor would have my head and my black card if I didn't hold to a secret. It's common knowledge that WikiLeaks was bad. Don't make me a part of Crowngate."

"Car."

She blows out a heavy breath. "Fuck. If I'm fired, I will murder you, Circe Maco."

"You won't murder me, you love me."

"Yeah, but you need me more for correct coffee runs, clothing and gossip."

"Then give me the gossip. Something miniscule." I'll plead. Not that it'll do me a lick of good, but I'll try anything. "I'll trade you shoes for information."

"Oh, come on! Circe, that's dirty warfare. Shoes are not to be used in such a way."

"Give me something, Carli. I'll tell the Governor about the Jell—"

"Don't you dare! No. You promised no one would know about that night. It was dark, it was dangerous, and I was not sober. You said girl code reined. Don't break it now." Striking the deep chords that make her fold, I bet I can get something with one more shot.

"What about the girl code? Are you trying to break it, Carli?"

"Fuck. Fuck. Fuck. Fuck. Fuckity assholes and sparkly dragons, you're a bitch. I love you. Your tactics are evil, Circe *Matcheson*." I can hear her failing.

Staying quiet, I wait. She's caving.

Waiting.

Waiting.

"Fine, but this is all you get and I'm hanging up. Take this as the only thing you get, and if you call me before things change in the media, I will swear, I won't answer the phone."

"I solemnly swear that I'm—"

"Yeah, yeah, HP. Hold off the oath. I'm saying it fast then hanging up. Ready?"

Quietly, hiding the phone uber close to the bed, in case Sali or the doc come in, I reply, "Yes."

"I'm going to get in so much shit. And if I'm missing in a few days, get bail ready. Oh! And Captain America."

Pausing further. The line is quiet, quiet, quiet.

"Someone died."

Hearing the resounding click of the line going dead, I can't move.

Leaving the receiver where it lies, I turn over without another thought and cry myself to sleep.

Chapter Twenty-Five

China

I'm pacing back and forth in the room, unsure of what to do.

"I'm hiding in a fucking broom closet, Har!"

"Get your shit together, CD. You knew you had a chance of running into her at some point. I had a running bet with Hallee that you'd see her by week three. You made me lose a thousand bucks!" Talking to Harlow always puts things into perspective. Well, sort of.

"You had a bet on when I'd run into Circe? You're fucking with me?"

Her high-pitched voice carries over the phone's speaker in the tiny space. "Fuck off. Don't act surprised, Uncle Buck. Of course, I did. We even have a running tally on when Casper will be awake too. Right now, Catty owes me five grand, and I'm hoping he keeps it up."

Fuck me. My friends are idiots. "Of course, you have running bets on shit like this."

"What else would we bet on? Whiskey isn't about to wake up at the snap of my fingers to fall in love with me, so I have to try and fleece my besties any way I can."

"So you haven't answered my question. What do I do? I mean, she doesn't know we're that close, and I don't want her to know yet. The last thing I need is someone else in the room worrying alongside me."

"At some point, you have to tell her."

"Not yet."

Flicking my nail on the handle of a broom, I listen to Harlow admonish me for being a pussy about my brother's girlfriend. "You can't hide out in a broom closet for weeks on end, so pick up those five hundred dollar undies—"

"Not wearing any today," I interrupt.

"That's my girl."

"I'd love to be, but Jamieson ditched me, and didn't bring me a jump bag."

"Oh. Well then, I'll go shop and bring you some goodies. Anything else you need for your tryst with the maintenance man?"

"Har har, harlot. No. Just bring me lunch and coffee. Make it a venti this time, cheapskate." Pulling open the door, peering around corner, I don't see Circe or her mother anywhere.

"Fine. But get me ten minutes alone with Whiskey in that broom closet, and I'll bring you a scone."

Closing the door, I head back to Wyatt's room. "Just get me a drink. And no more bets."

"No promises." Is the last thing she says before hanging up.

Pocketing my phone, I talk to myself on the way back to the room. "My friends are idiots."

Chapter Twenty-Six

Circe

Push yourself past the pain, they said. Deal with the loss and the regrets, they said. That was then. That was when I was dealing with the loss of Shelby and Kiresa. Moreover, the regret of being the one left behind. They say that when you are the only survivor in a plane crash, that out of two hundred people, the single survivor will have regrets and remorse. The why me? Why did I survive? What did I do that made me the lucky one?

That's what I lived with. That's what I endured as I learned to deal with the pain of being the one that still got to grow up. I was able to flounder through life and learn to be an adult. I'm the one that can live off of nine dollars a week to eat. I *learned* how I could be grateful for being the survivor.

That was the first time my life was eradicated and erased. My life changed in seconds. But, I picked my ass up off the hospital bed, the couch, the floor, and sucked up the regret, turning it into a burning need to accomplish something of worth.

This time, I think it might take a bit more. I've been going to physio and the pyscho-babble analyst to deal with my internal and external injuries for almost a full month since seeing China, and after hearing the words from Carli. The physio hasn't made the progress expected because I'm not whole anymore. There're too many broken pieces now.

With Kiresa and Shelby, I knew the outcome. They died and I knew that life would go on if I only tried. This time, I don't know where, how, or what is going on with Wyatt and Marca.

Seeing China, acting like I was a burden to her, not someone considered a friend of hers or her brothers, I feel barren inside. My soul is literally curling in on itself as it loses hope of seeing him again. Weeks passed. There have been no answers and it's killing me. Was I better off not knowing someone died? No, I wasn't.

Thinking about that day, reliving it over and over, analyzing it, picking it apart piece by minuscule piece, I'm searching for a sign, a pattern, a blip or a hope that I'll remember what happened.

Every time I close my eyes, I see the final moments. In therapy, they want me to relive it play by play, but it's too much. When I don't agree and do as they ask by 'sharing my feelings,' then I'm branded hysterical. That's when the drugs come back out in tiny little syringes, putting me back to sleep.

If Wyatt survived this, I will do *everything* in my power to make sure he's never drugged against his will again.

Chapter Twenty-Seven

Wyatt

W

yatt, this sucks hairy cat nuggets. There's nothing more I want than for you to wake your ass up. I'm not doing this alone," Doll mutters to herself as she's watching television.

Time is so out of sync as I flick through memories, like the stations China switches through. Hearing every minute sound, feeling everything like a ticking time bomb in my head. Nothing changes. If they leave me in my mind for much longer, I'll be a bigger mess than I was before. I *know* it.

Hearing the scuffle of people as they move around the tiny space, or when the alarms resounds with a horrific yelp to pierce the silence, I feel like a cat with my nails stuck on the blinds.

Daily, they're in the room switching over bedding, scraping chairs on the floor, opening and closing curtains, all to keep the perception of normalcy. As daylight streams in, it caresses my skin when it makes the hairs on my arm stick up. It keeps up the pretense that I'm alive. I'm not alive, I'm surviving.

Doll has spent every waking hour with me. I've yet to speak with her, nor have I opened my eyes, and I haven't been able to say thank you to her for being here. There's nothing I wish for more. *Nothing.*

I want to tell her what happened, how everything changed in seconds.

How the drive down was fine, the highway serene. Mother and I were more than fine. Hell, the day was fucking fantastic! A moment of clarity with refreshing dialogue was cordial, and I almost felt loved.

Our relationship had always been abrasive and volatile like an A-bomb. Constantly requiring interference from Dad, or from neatly filled syringes. That was our life together. Our relationship normally sucked, and I feel horrible that now Whiskey and Doll, especially Doll, have been robbed of feeling the same as I did that day. Dad would have been so happy to see it.

Dad.

Wow, there's a whole other regret. Sorrow for not being able to give him the peace of personally seeing it happen. To tell Doll there was laughter, joy, and peace at the end would seem incorrect, but it's true; we had peace. Yeah, that's it. We understood each other for however brief a moment it was.

We were conversing and acting like family should. We still hadn't really spoken about my new position then, and I'd thought about it a ton sitting here in this blank hallway of a mind, but I feel no better about it.

Thinking about home and that day, I see everything in my mind as if I'm there. The sun is just below the horizon, falling into the bright ocean. I can see the riptide as it rolls along the coast with the promise of days in the surf; downtime and relaxation after the will reading. Yes, I knew we'd be in for a few days of odd remarks, packing, tears, copious amounts of alcohol, and dangerous emotional implosions. Plus, there would be the silent diners where we'd all ignore the vacant seat at the table. I'd hoped for a bit of friendly competition with Doll on the track, and showing Circe that heaven. Most of all, I was looking forward to the joy on her face when I asked her the one thing I'd been afraid to ask. Because of all the circumstances surrounding us the past few weeks, I'd decided that she was what I wanted in my life. She's mine, and I won't give her up. Knowing it in my heart that first day, it's been the same every day. She consumes me.

"Has there been any changes?" Doll asks, knocking me out of my silent musings.

"Sorry, no. The doctor is still concerned with swelling. She'll keep him in the coma for a few more days, I suppose." The voice is elderly, kind sounding for sure, and soft, like what I'd expect a grandparent to sound like. It's Margaret, my stand-in nurse when Sali is off.

"Is there anything I can get for you?" Feeling the blanket on the bed being moved up my body, someone tucks it under my arms. It's odd in a way. After checking the IV line in my hand and puffing up the pillow a bit, they move away.

"No. I'm good, really." Doll sounds so worn out and exhausted. "Whiskey went out to get me a jump bag full of things again today. If I find he packs like a man and forgets something crucial, *again*, I'll reach out to you. Thanks."

Hearing the lady leave, closing the door behind her, the chair beside the bed shifts, scraping across the floor. Flicking her shoes off, propping her legs on the side of the bed, I feel her slight weight relax against mine.

"Wyatt, I've had enough of this. This shit is getting fucking old, and you need to wake up." Her cool feet rest up against mine as she tucks them under the light blankets. "I'm friggin' twenty-one in a few weeks, and I'm not gonna take much more of you avoiding me. So..." With her soft voice cracking, choking on her words, she's wipes tears away from her face. I know she's reaching the end of her emotional patience. Doll doesn't cry; she doesn't do emotions. "Big brother, get your ass back to me so I can beat your lazy butt on the track."

You bet your tiny little bumblebee ass I'll beat you, kid. This is shit, and I'm fully bored of it too. Whiskey is so much older than her, and honestly, he's more an uncle than a brother. Here I am, the one that she normally leans on, sitting in a drug-induced coma with no one else to help her cope. How is she keeping her calm and composed demeanor?

Skipping that thought, my mind drags me back to my Siren. I want to ask Doll about Circe. How is she? I *know* in my veins she was alive, barely, when I last saw her, but she was alive. That was before I passed out. Actually, I guess it wasn't so much passed out as it was more *died* for a short period of time.

How is it she's not here? She was beside me during all the craziness with Dad. Why isn't she here now?

And really, *how* is Doll fairing? Is Whiskey helping her? Is he keeping her sane and busy, so that she has no time to realize how crappy this is? I hope to fuck he's helping her. If not, I'm going to kick his ass when I wake the fuck up. We've had a shit run of luck in the past few months, and Doll's been rather grown-up through the whole experience. I've heard Whiskey talking to me a few times, but it's not really anything that could tell me how he's helping, how he's coping with this himself.

All of these thoughts swim like sharks in my mind. Dangerous, and not really accomplishing anything of real value. I guess I'll just have to wait.

There's more questions than answers, and no one can hear me.

Chapter Twenty-Eight

Wyatt

M

ore days blend, bend, and bow. How many have passed? The beeping monitor tells me nothing. There's no phone I can glance at, no one that will answer my internal musings; no one but me. If I start answering my own questions, I know I'm good and fucked.

Right now, I'm caged, alone, and really hitting the end of my proverbial rope. I'm stuck in the rubber room, banging on the padding with my arms stretched out, dangerously entwined in tight cloth wrapping around me. I'm fucking chained. That's how it *feels*.

Dark. Dank. Horrid. This cage of mine is worse than anything a psyche ward could ever envision.

Placing a person who feels every emotion to an excess in a straining situation, in their own personal jail, *that's* cruel fucking punishment. It's claustrophobic, cramped, and constrained in here. I'm fucking drowning in Wyatt. The memories, the disillusioned family ties, the sadness, disasters of days gone by, fucking crap I hoped to bury and hide away from the world. All of it swims to the surface, drowning my sanity. Doing everything I possibly can, I try holding it together, but I can't see myself keeping this up. My mind will be a tortured pig lead to slaughter soon.

Let me out! Screaming at the top of my lungs is futile. They think what they're doing will help and it won't.

Quiet is worse than noise.

How much longer can they keep me in this dangerous space with no contact, no conversation, and no way to dull the ache of the voices. They chatter, telling me I'm not good enough, I'm not the rightful person to control the business that Dad created, and that I'm a disgrace. That my proclivities just make me more dangerous to their public personas.

This was his to do! This was meant to be Dad's. It was never meant to be my future. With him gone, I'm afraid. A deep-seeded fear of showing my illness in public scares me the most. All I want to do is curl up in the corner, cuddling my sides, rocking away the stress of this.

FUCK!!!!

I want to give up, but I ignore the doubt of being nowhere good enough for the position they've given me, because I can't fix it. I tell myself to be strong, to hold out just a bit more and to control the cracks in the dyke, staunching the flow of my internal disaster.

It doesn't work.

I need Siren. She can fix me.

I need out of here.

I need out *now*.

I want no more of this blackness, no more dangerous thoughts.

Wyatt may be the broken one, but Casper fucking Crown bows to no one, let alone his own fucking head games.

Time to go, boys. I'm finding the door and leaving this hell. Now, where were those fucking keys?

Chapter Twenty-Nine

Wyatt

All day it's been like watching old family films, slides of long ago trips from the forties, or finding an old journal that was filled in by a grandparent. It's from a lifetime ago; it feels historic. I know my own head well enough that if I focus only on the negative, I'll be warring with myself. Like screaming down a long tunnel at no one, or being lost in a labyrinth without a string to find the exit. I'll get lost. It's stories that feel so real because of the emotions portrayed and conveyed will trap me. They've been flipping by so fast, I can't grasp them.

It's nothing more than snippets, like a fast scrolling video. You get the gist of the story, but it's sped up. Remembering days when we were at home, dealing with Mother, days of joy on the track, and losses as I learned to be conservative with my words. All of it's damning. Dealing with my own convoluted mind has been difficult. When this is done, either I'll have further cracks in my psyche, or I'll be a slave to it no more.

Our parents' mansion had its privileges. The days on the track when it was calm and peaceful helped. Being stuck here, inside this trash compactor of a brain I own, it's bike wreckage and shards of joy. The longer I'm here, the less I'll be sane on the other side. I know it. I feel it deeply.

Wading through catalogues full of times on the track, I'm remembering another time that was joyous. Doing this keeps the despair at bay.

The day is warm and inviting. The steaming Californian air is thick. Even the birds in the nearby palms are hiding under leaves to stay cool in the midday sun. It's perfect in every way. This is the perfect time to hit the track. The heat and the humidity from the ocean, the salt gums up the track. Both Dad and Doll say it's ludicrous, and I love it.

Hopping over the concrete stanchion that lines the track, landing on the heated blacktop that is my life, I'm happy.

This is where I live.

Knowing every inch of it and then some, I pick up a pebble and roll it between my fingers. Today is different. I feel it, somethings off. I need this. The ability to the ride the rim of each tight, solid, and unforgiving curve, hugging it tight to my chest until I feel I can't breathe from the closeness. *That's* perfection.

Today, I feel them. The ghosts loom on the track as palpable entities. They're always here, waiting, wishing for another try to best me. They're the ghosts of my past. Times when I failed, times when I bested my own records, or times when I felt the need to push the envelope a tad bit further. It's frightening. When no one's here, you can hear them creep around the corners, swerving to miss a danger that only they can see.

I see them. I've always seen them. Sometimes they were imagined. Sometimes, though, they were strong specters that slid up behind you to make you go faster, pushing you to your limits until you almost do too much. Dad always said, "*A good racer feels the nuances of the track, that you can anticipate the point when you'll lose it. A great racer knows how to make the track work for them. You won't have to feel it, you'll just know.*"

He was right. You *feel* when it's right.

Kneeling, leaning my back against the cool concrete, I pull up a seat. The gravel on the track's edge is a combination of tar, rubber, flicks of rock that are kicked up, and sweat from our personal vehicles of choice.

"Do you see it, Wyatt?" My dad asks. Looking up to his massive form, I see the joy, the passion he has for us, and the care for the track's ghosts that have bested him too.

"Not today," I say mechanically, almost rehearsed.

"Wyatt, it's always there. You just have to grab it." He's talking about visualizing the cup in my hand.

Remembering this conversation, we sat here and talked the day before my first TT race. He was sure I could do it, whereas I was scared I'd disappoint.

"You just have to visualize the win. Don't *feel* that it can't happen, because it won't if you can't. Can't is a shit answer to anything." Laughing at this, tossing a rubberized rock, it skips across the surface of the track like a pebble on a flat pond.

"I know. Can't is for pussies. I'm no pussy, Dad. I *can* do it. I'm just afraid of not bringing my best, disappointing you with my performance."

Laughing, he ruffles my hair. "I love you, Wyatt. I'm never disappointed in you."

Wanting to enjoy this trip down memory lane, soaking up the moment I had with my father, I know it's not real. He's just another ghost of the track now.

And as soon as I think that, he disappears, leaving me to sit on the edge of this quiet track alone. I wish he were still alive. I need a moment more of his time. It's a cold reminder that he's gone. He was gone too fast. *Way, way too fast.*

Needing him with me, needing him to help me find my way through this, his loving and caring soul could've helped me work through this, whatever it is.

Not wanting to leave the stillness of this moment, I take it in, exhaling deeply.

The track hums with anticipation. It's waiting for me to hit the blacktop. It wants my rubber to slip across its surface. Come dance with the devil, it says. It's calling for me.

There's almost nothing I'd rather have...almost.

Wanting to run to the garage, slipping the bike out of its soft and warm paddock, I ache to make it screech in joy as we kiss the rim of death. But it's not real.

What is real? Siren. She's real, Dad is not.

Internalizing it to myself, I feel the weight of the truth. The track escapes in a dreamlike fog, the warm air with the sweet moisture of the ocean, and the light of day beaming sunshine dulls to a dim hue. It's shocking, seeing it dissipate. That warmth, the comfort of the track, and Dad's love as it surrounded me, all of it's gone. I know without a doubt I'm back in my own mind. In in the hospital bed, in my cranial trap.

Enough! No more! Dad's words ring out, that I need to dust it off and get up. I can't stay here any longer. Shaking off the cloud of the past, I immediately notice the lights of the hospital's sterile room. They're gross and unloving as I lazily open my eyes. Doll's long chocolate hair is strewn around her face, partially covering, partially hanging down the side of the awkward chair. Sitting propped up with a blanket tucked around her shoulders, her legs are curled under her uncomfortably in a reclined position. I feel bad for everything she's endured. She looks so worn out, so tired, and it seems like she's aged years since I physically saw her last.

Stirring awake, I attempt speech. My mouth is parched like the Mojave, and the best I can muster is a deep groan. Coughing lightly, grunting, and generally humph a few unrecognizable noises, it wakes Doll.

Sitting up so fast, the blanket she was hidden under is tossed off, discarded like trash. But it's that look. The look on her face is priceless. Appearing at my side with a massive grin, she says, "What took you so long?" She's clearly relieved to see me awake.

Reaching down to the floor, picking up the castaway blanket, she drapes it across my body as her tears flow down her face. "I've missed the shit out of you." Controlling the bed, righting me to a sitting position, she hits the button for the nurse, frantically.

"Water, D." Squeaking it out, she grabs it fast, handing it to me in a blink.

Pushing the button for the nurse a few more times, she doesn't stop grinning. Holding the cup up to me, I'm sip it slowly. The water feels amazing in my dry mouth. Pulling it through the straw, I relish the ache it assuages as it passes down my throat. Working up the best smile I can with a sore jaw, cottontail mouth, and rough inner cheeks, Doll pulls the cup away as I release the straw. When we crashed, I must have bit down hard, as the sores on the inside of my mouth are still tender.

Within seconds, the tiny room becomes a flurry of activity. The gentle doctor and elderly nurse that I'd heard before become real people. They shuffle around my inactive body, checking monitors and such as I allow the ministrations.

Pushing the cup back to me, as I'm sipping at the straw, the lovely older nurse asks, "You must be feeling better?"

Trying to smile, she pulls my hand out of the covers to check my pulse. Her touch is slightly cool, but refreshing as she tracks the beats on her watch. Once satisfied with the results, she places my hand back on the bed, covers it with the half-warm flannel, then turns to write it in the log sheets.

"I'll check back in a bit. I'm sure you have things to talk about. If you need me, just ring, China." Smiling as she exits the room, she closes the door to the outside noises. The doctor stays for a moment more.

Going over the chart, still checking monitors, smiling at Doll and I, she says, "Glad you made it back, sugar. It would be a harmful waste to lose something as precious as you." She smiles wide. "I have to pull my rounds, but I'll be back in just a tick." She leaves Doll and I in a companionable silence.

Instinctively hopping up on the bed, Doll tucks into my side, assuming the position we've had since we were kids. I'm tired, but I don't care. We need to talk. Man, I missed this.

"Where's Whiskey?" I mumble. Figuring it's not nice to go for the gullet yet, I wonder where our older, flightier brother is.

"He should be back soon. He went out to check on something. He's tight-lipped as usual. There's a backstory, but I don't care. I've had enough to worry about with just your mug stuck in a coma. PS, thanks for that. Like I didn't need more trouble these past few months."

I think about what she said. Months? Fuck. I didn't realize it'd been *that* long. Dreams and reality blended as I was tucked away in my own mind. Deciding to avoid that conversation for the moment, and getting to heart of what I want to know, I ask, "How is she?"

Doll takes a deep breath, sighs, and expels the pent-up stressful breath. This was imminent.

"She's alive. She's sore, broken, and worried sick about you, but..." She turns over to her side, propping herself on her elbow to peer down at me. "I haven't really dealt with that. Sorry, Cas. The nurses asked my permission to tell her, but I asked that they hold off until we saw about your recovery. My first priority was you." Her composure is thinning as the strain drains from her face. She's had to grow up so fast, in such a short period of time. Almost twenty-one, and she's been in charge of my care, my well-being, and I'm sure in family affairs that she honestly had no business caring for.

"I'm sorry, Doll. This shouldn't have been your burden." Talking even this much is straining my vocal cords. Sure, I'd been idle in the coma, but I'm exhausted awake, if that makes sense.

She pets my chest, kisses my forehead and smiles. "It's not your fault. Now that you're awake, things will change, I'm sure. Your stubborn streak will shine through, Cas. So get strong, get your ass out of bed and help me. Then I'll forgive you." After a quirky smile, she rolls off the bed. "I'll go see what's taking Whiskey so long with my lunch. Just relax, okay?"

Nodding, she pulls the blanket up tight to my chest. Bending down to place her shoes on and heads to the door. "I love you, Cas."

God, I love her too. "Ditto, kid. See you in a bit."

Chapter Thirty

Wyatt

Needing to tell Doll and Whiskey the whole story from beginning to end is paramount. Waking yesterday, I went back to sleep almost immediately, but it felt good to know I could wake up now on my own. I've been awake now for the last three hours, and it feels like my insides are jumping to get loose. My mental shell is falling to rubble in a pile of soft marshmallowy goo. My body is loose, my mind is wired, and my impatient soul wants to get out. I want to find Siren.

But I have a priority. Doll and Whiskey *need* to know what happened first. The nurses and doctors have been checking my pulse, heart rate, blood count, eyesight, cognitive recollection and every other motion my body can make. Doll sat perfectly still in the chair, watching as Dr. Callie, the nurses, and every other intern needing to see the effects of coma recovery. Most have left now, leaving only the doctor, Doll, Whiskey and I in the silence, waiting for the elephant in the room to take over.

"I want to check on you in a few hours, and you've only just come back so please, please, do me favor and get more rest. It seems redundant to sleep after a coma, but even though you've been out cold for a bit, you need it." She loops her stethoscope around her neck then walks to the door, closing it tightly behind her.

Kicking back in the chair, Doll relaxes to a point. Whiskey in no way is relaxed. Legs crossed at the ankles, leaning on the wall, he looks ready to pounce.

"Okay, I'll start this." Doll shifts forward in the chair, slings her feet across my bed and smirks. "So, deets before you go back to snooziepoo land."

I'm finding it hard to not laugh at that. I've been sitting here in *snooziepoo land*, as she put it, waiting to speak to her about it all. I guess now is as good a time as any.

Patting the bed beside me, Doll hops up off the chair and curls up in the corner "Whiskey, Sit, man. You're killing me."

With a stern scowl, he shakes his head. "Nah. I'm good here."

Fine. "So, you know I promised Mother that I would come and stay at the house until the family celebration for Dad. I thought I could handle her. I thought I could handle the soul-crushing sadness, and the pall of disappointment that hangs around me when I'm within her wrath."

"Yeah, kind of been there for all of that, Wyatt. I was just smart enough to head out and hide in public, away from her scrutiny that day. Which I'm kicking myself for now."

"Don't feel bad. You were doing what you could to survive *us*." I always wondered what I did to gain my mother's undying hatred and display of incredulous disdain. I was always fearful to ask, but now I know better. Our relationship was strained because of our commonalities.

"When you popped out to shop with the girls, you left me to deal with the despair as she boxed up Dad's things."

Handing me the glass of water off the table beside the bed, I sip at it, watching as they await my diatribe. I'm sort of stalling.

Doll sets the glass back down. "Cas?"

"Yeah, Doll?"

"Look, I get it. You just woke up, and I'm not rushing you. Trust me, I know you need time." She gets it so easily. She understands better than I ever expected.

"Maybe a bit more sleep," I say as she tucks the blanket back up around my chin. "Then I'm all yours, okay?"

"Yeah. That sounds good." Kissing my forehead, she rises off the bed with a perfect smile. I've been waiting to see that. "Sleep, then spill. K, Cas?"

I'm quiet for a second as she takes in my tired state. Smiling back at her, she grabs a sweater off the chair, exiting with Whiskey in tow.

Not knowing how long this recovery will be, I don't doubt how hard a go I have ahead of me. I've watched it enough with other racers as bones mend. I'm not worried about bones.

It's the mental state that will kill me.

Chapter Thirty-One

China

Finally. That's all I could think.

Finally, he's awake. Finally, he's back.

We still haven't gone over the accident, what happened, what's gone on since he was in the coma, and everything in-between. Thing was, I needed out way too badly. If I didn't blow this prison, I was going to lose my shit on someone. I need a moment alone to release the stress and the joy I'm feeling. After Wyatt went back to sleep, and Whiskey said he'd stay behind, I knew there was someone to watch him.

Almost running down the stairs, taking off like a bat out of hell, I peeled out of the long-term parking as fast as my fingers could hold the throttle on my 1250cc road monster. I'm so grateful that Whiskey brought out my ride. Sure, it was torture for a few days, realizing it was out there, waiting for me as I was stuck inside. But I finally got to escape. Whiskey will look after Cas. Casper promised to wait for me before he went over things so the two of them can catch up on guy shit. When I come back, I won't have to listen to bro crap.

With Wyatt sleeping in that awful coma, I never left. In my heart, I knew it was taking its toll on all of us. If I could get out on the highway to let the bike loose, shaking out the cobwebs, then maybe I'd find a bit of peace before I heard the truth of it all. Feeling there's a dreadful story to be told, I'll need a bit of zen to deal with it.

Passing through the UCLA campus, I felt more relaxed than I had in weeks, and I swear I was breathing a bit easier too. This is what I needed.

Sitting on the bike, rolling my shoulders and stretching out my body, inevitably everything argues and pushes back. After sitting in that crap-ass folding death trap for close to two months, I've become stiff and sore. Dr. Callie, in all her infinite Southern Belle sweetness, felt bad for me a few weeks back. Giving me a pass to the staff's sparse gym, I was able to get in a run on the ancient treadmill and lift a few weights to clear my head. The last thing I wanted was to become the soft marshmallow like I watched Wyatt slowly turn in to. After the days turned into weeks, I knew he was going to need physio, and loads of it. I didn't want to be like him. I needed to get off my duff. It wouldn't help my damaged soul, but for sure, it might keep me from going batshit crazy sitting in that nine-by-nine cell.

Advancing on the lights at the corner, I wait to turn onto Wiltshire Blvd. Traffic is subdued this time of day, which is good. I won't have to fight commuters.

Reaching back and sky high, I push the muscles in my back to lengthen as I shake out my knots.

"Fuck, I needed this," I mutter as I twist back and forth, then side to side, stretching everything out.

It feels fantastic.

This *day* is fantastic. Fuck, even the sun is shining brighter.

The warmth of it is amazing on my skin, recharging me better than any shopping could. The fetid smell of the inner-city smog seems diminished, and it's almost tolerable as I take in all the noise around me. It's as if they are integral in orchestrating my freedom.

I don't care that the cars honk because of impatient drivers on phones, and I care even less that the impolite assholes have no idea how to drive. Each ignore the lights so they can rush past me and my bike before the red hits. If any of these morons ever got behind the handles of my machine, they'd pee themselves. The feeling of the horses letting loose on the sweaty blacktop is the best sensation on earth to me, and not one of these asses can say the same inside their steel boxes.

The light flicks green as I cautiously wait to turn. Like I said, I know there'll be some moron wanting to scream through the light like a banshee. After checking the way is clear a couple times, I pull onto Wiltshire, heading out toward the highway. Out there, I'll be able to stretch the speed as I weave in and out of traffic.

On a bike, I'm fearless. There's nothing about regular traffic that scares me. I pass on the left in a space that could only fit a stroller, and I increase, not decrease, my speed as I come into a curve. Brakes are only used in grand emergencies. The freeway is a piece of cake.

Merging into the next lane, I follow along behind the perfect example of a distracted driver—a mother in a minivan. I know I won't be safe here. She's more likely to reach for something she shouldn't, veering off into the opposing lane and causing instant mayhem and carnage. So, before I become roadkill, I quickly shift, pulling in behind a sleek black Lambo. The best part of tailing high-end cars is that no one wants to be responsible for the insurance claims. They avoid them at all costs. Thankfully, becoming my perfect traffic buffer.

Sailing through lights, passing under the overpass for the 405, my cavalcade escapes into a side street, leaving me an unprotected, Bouncing Betty once more. Increasing my speed slightly, I pass a few trucks.

Swinging onto the Interstate, I let loose the evil screaming engine. Pulling into the flow opposite the direction of our house. My family home now holds nothing for me. There's no love, no obligations, and no controlling forces to direct me to their will. I'll be totally free soon. With Wyatt back, and me creeping up on my twenty-first birthday, which is only mere weeks away, I have less constraints. *Weeks*, that's it. My race proceeds will be released into my control. My inheritance will be freed up, and my trust fund that was hung over my head for years will be mine to decide. Sure, they tried to hold it to twenty-five, but death rearranged that. I'm not looking to spend it on wild nights and hookers, but I want the control of deciding my fate in this world where my family is broken and distended.

Concentrating on the road, the highway is smooth, light, and utterly incredible. It's just what the doctor ordered. Even though I've grown up in Santa Monica boutiques, Malibu bodegas, and lived off Rodeo Drive cafés or restaurants for as long as I can remember, I feel more at ease here. Following the traffic until we come into the part of town I want, I'm running into LA's seedier section. It's dirty, unkempt, smelly, and nowhere here would you find a Prada or Fendi. This isn't an area you'd normally find someone such as me either. If mother saw me...well, let's just say I'm out of place by her standards, but fully in my element. She never really understood me. I know these streets better than anything near my home.

Sweeping past minivans and trucks, zipping in-between wannabe racers with their costly tuned cars, every passing second I feel the tension lifting.

Fuck, I missed this. I never realized how badly I needed to be on the two-wheeled heathen. Leaning into the turn for the off-ramp, I swing right. I pull up beside an unmarked car with his darkened windows. I'm wearing my mirrored visor, so I know he can't see me as well as he'd like. It's probably causing him a coronary. Cops hate the unknown. Honestly, I don't give a fuck.

Revving the engine, causing the highly-tuned devil to snap and lurch in its place, I smile. Even though I have full control, and I'll take off from the light slowly, it's a blast to crank them up.

Watching the signal for the opposing traffic, the light's about to change. Flicking the throttle once more, causing the bike to sing its glee, I await the sign to go. Prepping my hands, bouncing on the balls of my feet, the bike rocks and spits to race away at a moment's notice. It screams to me—*Once that light changes, I'm off like a shot,* it says. I'm sure it'll cause them to check my plate. Any expensive bike on Crenshaw causes a stir.

It's funny, really. No one expects a petite girl behind the mask, and no one expects *me.* They always anticipate some punk ass loser that's boosted some rich kid's ride. I've been pulled over more than I like. It's comical. When they realize it's me, the racing darling, the charges are normally dropped, sometimes.

Street racing charges stick. Only thing now, there's no dad to get the calls, and no mom to freak out if she ever learned about it. The only one who'd even give a flying monkey's ass about it is Wyatt. He'll accommodate my need for release, and help me deal with things.

Fuck, it's mainly his fault anyway. If it wasn't for him introducing me and getting me hooked like heroine on motorcycles, then I would've had another hobby arranged by my mother. More piano, ballet, knitting, and fucking tennis.

God, I *hated* tennis.

Looking over at the cop car once more before leaving the light, I smile to myself. Hitting the throttle, releasing the brake and clutch, I advance onto the road, watching the cop vaguely in my peripheral. Switching lanes, I pull down the street just ahead of him, trying to blend in around the various mundane drivers. Clearing my head in the breeze and passing the time is all I want. Trouble is the last thing I need today.

Turning on my blinker, entering the center lane, I ready to turn onto the side street that will take me away from his watchful eye. This will take me back toward the hospital, where hopefully, Wyatt is ready to go over things. I'm itching to know the story, but afraid to hear the truth. What a double-edged sword.

Just before clicking the throttle again, the chirp of a siren rings out. It's just once, but enough to make me look in the mirror.

Fuck me. The cop followed. For shit's sake.

His lights engage, the siren chirps a couple more times as he's telling me to pull off to the side of the road. Awaiting him for whatever infraction he feels I committed, I shut off the bike. Flicking the kickstand, removing the strap on my chin, I unclasp the button at my neck on the jacket. Moving, I don't mind the tightness of the warm leather, but stopped, it's a bit constricting in the heat. Leaning back on the seat, I wait. I hear the car door open and close. Chatting into his com, he makes his way toward me. Stepping up, looking down in that condescending smirk that I'm so used to seeing, I doubt this will be any different than any other time before. More often than not, they feel shorted when they find out I'm too much trouble.

"Please remove your helmet," he says in a clipped tone.

Smiling, I lift the visor, then pull the helmet off. Shaking out my hair, I grab my sunglasses from the inner pocket of my coat and loop my helmet across the handlebar. I don't turn to face him yet. The last thing I want to do is give him a reason to give me grief. Time is not on my side right now, and the mood I'm in, I'll probably give him a hard time. More than a sixty percent chance, I'd say.

"Yes, officer?"

Clearing his throat, he reaches for his note pad and pen. "Do you know why I stopped you, miss?"

Miss? Are you shitting me. "Nope. Not a clue, *sir*," I quip back sarcastically.

"You have a taillight out."

"You must be joking?" Flicking the indicator, I pop up off the seat, stepping off on the curbside, walking around to look.

Fuck.

"Really, you've gotta be shitting me," I mutter to myself. "Fucking Whiskey couldn't even look at it before riding it over." Tapping the light, I see it faintly flicker before it goes out completely.

"No need to swear, miss." Opening the pad, he starts writing notes, all while I cuss like a trucker under my breath.

Bloody brother, I'll make him pay for this ticket.

"I'm so sorry, Officer. I haven't ridden in weeks, and I didn't realize it was out." I'm short with him, as I just want to be on my way. "I have some place to be, so if you could just write the ticket, I'll be off to let you enjoy your afternoon." I look at him and take in the man who's ruined my high. He's actually quite handsome. A bit older, maybe mid-twenties, and well kept. With wide shoulders, a tight chest that thins down to his cinched, belted waist, and long shapely legs. I like what I see. Checking him out without looking up higher, I'm not really a girl for the upper parts. Hairless chests and trimmed man bits suit me just fine.

"Remove your glasses, please," he says tightly.

Frig! I guess I'm not leaving here quickly.

I pull them down, but I don't remove them. Finally, I look up into his face, which is scruff free. He's wearing a pair of mirrored glasses, just like the ones from that old TV show CHIPS that I watched while bored in the hospital. They frame his face nicely. Hard chin with a tiny mole on the corner of his pouty lips, mousey blonde hair that's almost shoulder length, and a hole in his ear where a spacer would usually sit. It's not a large space, but defined enough to notice.

"License and registration, please."

"Of course." God dammit. Shit. Shit. Shit.

Reaching into my seat locker, I produce the papers and complete my perusal of him as he looks them over. His chin has a slight puckered scar, and the sharp cheekbones and tight muscles tick in his jaw as he looks down at me.

Go figure. I've pissed off yet another cop.

"Did you know this is out of date?" He lifts up the ownership papers, pointing out the expiration on my insurance.

Snapping it out of his hands, I bring it close to my face. "Oh, mutha!"

The freaking date is the day before dad died. I haven't seen any of this. I never had to worry about any of it before, and if Whiskey was half the brother he should've been, I wouldn't be driving with an expired fucking registration.

"No reason to swear." He holds out his hand for the ownership, starting off to the car. "Please step to the curb, ma'am. I'll be right back." I hear him under his breath mutter, "Of all the stops, on any shift, it had to be me. Are you fuckin' kidding."

Pulling out my phone, I dial Jamieson. It rings, and rings, *and rings.*

Fuck me.

Of course the one time I need his ass most, he doesn't answer me. I'm about to try my girls, then consider it's wiser to keep them out of it. It's not like I can call Circe, even though I know she'd help me. Well, maybe not so much right now. I kept her away from Casper. I'm pooched. The best I can do is take the ticket, smile, and hop back on as fast as I possibly can. Then beat the shit out of Whiskey when I see him.

Looking back to the police officer as he sits in the car, he looks up at me periodically as he writes the ticket. Speaking into his com system, I try Whiskey again. Reclining back on the curb, thinking about all the shitty things I'll do to him, the cop exits his car, still talking into his shoulder com. As his phone rings, his shoulders slump, and I swear I hear him hiss a reply before he answers the call.

"Yes, sir. No, of course. Yes." Is all I can hear of the conversation while he stands by the far side. With a swift 10-4, he hangs up the phone and makes his way back over to me.

"Miss," he states, rather taut. He walks with a purpose, one that I'm not sure I wish to know. Why does he look like I'm in more trouble than I think?

"Yes, officer," I say as sweetly. I have a way with people, and most times I use it to my advantage. Right now, I have the feeling it won't work in my favor.

"There are outstanding tickets that haven't been processed and paid out. I'm going to have to ask you to come with me."

"The fuck?"

"Miss, I'm going to have your bike impounded, and you'll have to come with me. There are outstanding violations that you're wanted for, and it seems you didn't appear in court last week on two of them. The judge has sent an order of detainment. You'll have to come with me. I'm sorry." He steps up beside me, pulling out his cuffs, and I have an overwhelming need to rant.

"You're shitting me right now, right?" Stepping back from him, I toss my arms in the air. I'm pissed.

This. Is. Shit.

Unlatching the first cuff, flicking it against my upraised wrist, he proceeds to turn me around, gently, before adding the second bracelet. I'm small in size compared to him, even though I'm just shy of six feet. And I'd say he holds a good hundred pounds on me. My argument will be short-lived.

"Really? I'm being arrested? This has got to be the worst fucking joke ever."

"Not a joke, Miss Crown." Turning me so that I'm facing him, he lifts off my glasses, hooks them in my jacket pocket and pulls the key from my bike.

"I can't believe I have to do this," he mutters again. He pulls himself up to his full height. He has a professional air of superiority in his demeanor. "You have the right to remain silent. You have the right to an attorney," he says as he turns me toward the rear door, still speaking in deep tones.

Really, I don't hear much after that as I'm still trying to process the idea that I've been arrested. As I'm led toward the back seat of a cruiser by a good-looking cop, my mind swims with the idea that my brother, who just woke up, won't know of this. My other brother, who didn't have the decency to answer his fucking phone, won't know that I'm about to be printed and set in a jail cell. I'll have to await his prissy butt to release me. Fucking great.

Placing me in the back before silently hopping in, the officer seems affected by this. He's not my problem, though. Watching in quiet detachment as I'm being driven off in cuffs, my perfectly gorgeous bike is left on the side of the road in West LA. I'll be lucky if they find any parts of it left to put into impound. Something as pretty as her will be parted out in fifteen minutes or less.

Turning the car around, passing my bike and heading toward the station for processing, I may not have turned twenty-one yet, but I'm about to find out the hard way what it means to be an adult.

Chapter Thirty-Two

Wyatt

It's been a few hours. You sure you haven't heard from her?" I ask Whiskey for the third time since waking up from another nap. Shaking his head, he pulls out his phone and shows me the screen; no missed calls. Weird.

Deciding to change topics, moving onto other things, Jamieson and I catch up on things unrelated to the accident. "How's things on the circuit?"

He paces the floor of the room, scuffing his feet along the tiles as he ponders his answer carefully. "I was pulled from the team."

"You're shittin' me. Why?"

"You, ya dumbass. I couldn't be at the practices. I can't very well hit the slopes in sunny fucking California. China needed me so bad that I couldn't leave her alone for a second." He pulls up the chair that Doll's been sleeping in and reclines it back. "Plus, to be honest, I couldn't fucking keep my head in the game when I was worrying about your melon, you stupid bastard."

I laugh at that. "Could you find two or three more cuss words to add to that sentence, or were you full up."

Pulling the handle a tad more, shifting the chair, his smile is genuine. "Stupid, fucking, little shit. That better?"

"Perfect. Thanks." Reaching for my unexplainable lunch that they left, eating the only thing I find edible, I quickly push the table away.

"You gotta eat more than goddamn Jell-O, you puss. Do you want me to order in like China's been doing for weeks on end?"

Smart fucking girl. "Yeah, I'm craving a cheeseburger from Patties. Think you could manage that?"

Nodding his head, he rises out of the dingy recliner. "Pussy. I'll grab us a couple, and fries too. You still want that mayo shit on it?"

"Yes, mayo shit would be fucking fantastic, asshole." Which grants me a larger than life Dad deep laugh. I miss that shit.

"Fine, mayo shit it is. There's one here on campus. I'll be back in a bit."

Chapter Thirty-Three

Jamieson

Go get me a fucking burger he says." I grumble while I pass a few doctors on the way to the elevators. Everyone is so tiny, and so fucking wasteful in their appearance. China told me Wyatt's doctor gave her access to the gym. It's for certain that no one here uses it. There must be a thick coat of dusting everywhere. In a zombie apocalypse, every one of these soft marshmallow puffheads wouldn't live; they'd all be dead.

Stupid fucks. Dumb ass lazy cunts, all of them.

Every chance I've had, I slung my ass back to the house just to hit the gym. Going and getting Doll clothing was the perfect excuse to head out there. Obviously, that's why I let the *house witch* pack her clothes instead of asking one of her girlfriends to do it. Plus, I know it's safer than being around her friends. Nutbars, all of them.

As I wait, one of the other assholes standing at the elevator bank has already selected the bottom floor. Watching as it descends from the top floor toward us, at the excessive speed of 'fuck all,' I try to find some calm in my demeanor before I commit murder. Most times, I give in and take the stairs, but today I'm in no rush, as the woman that holds all my thoughts is out of town dealing with her own family bullshit. No use in flying down flights. It would just cause my chubby to ache with the want of her tight loving pussy that's nowhere in sight. Just when I thought that staying in LA would get monotonous, I ran into her. Checking out board wax for her boogie board at Powder Kings. Watching her argue with Pete about something and schooling him on his perusal of her tits, I found it quite entertaining.

Just thinking about her short pink hair, piercing brown eyes and sinful body, gives me a wicked need for release.

Fuck. Now I have to stand here and will it under control.

Stupid idiot.

"Pardon?" I hear the puissant doctor beside me say.

Glaring at him, looking down upon a man that, well, if you call four foot nothing a man, he's nothing more than a soft noodle. "What's your problem, asshole?" I ask.

"You," he stammers. "You called me a stupid idiot."

Good going, James. Scare the little man.

Shit.

"Sorry," I say quietly, without crassness or cynicism. "I didn't mean that to you."

He nods his thanks for the apology, then moves over a step. Standing there in uncomfortable silence, awaiting the final few flights of the elevator's ascent, my phone pings. Pulling it out of my jeans, immediately the screen lights up with three missed calls. One's from Cassidy, the house witch. Thank fuck I missed that one. One is from China with no message. The last one left a message from an unknown number about an hour ago. Shit, there's no signal near Wyatt's room.

Hitting the button, I listen. "You are in so much, so, so, *soooo* much trouble for not answering my calls. I'm at district seven booking using my single call. Get your ass over here. *Don't. Tell. Wyatt.*" Playing it back again, China's at the police station just off Crenshaw. Why?

"What the fuck are you doing there?" I ask myself. Really, I don't get it, but I guess I better go find out.

The guy at the elevator looks at me with that same strange, scared rabbit look as before as I turn on my heel. Spinning back to the nurse's station and toward Wyatt's room, I dial Patties and place our order. Making my way back to his room, his nurse, Sali, is just coming around the corner.

"Excuse me."

She stops and gives me a sweet smile. "Yes, Mr. Crown?" Fuck, I still hate hearing that.

"I have to run out. Could you please let my brother know I'll be back in a bit?" I hand her fifty bucks. "I've order him something that should arrive shortly. Would you please give this to the delivery kid?"

"Sure, I can do that, Mr. Crown." No matter how many times I hear that, it hurts like fuck. Dad was Mr. Crown, and I'm just Jamieson, the fucked-up son that was shipped out.

"No offence, but your hospital food is shit." Handing her the money, I move off toward the stairs.

I hear her as I'm walking away. "Oh, we know."

Chapter Thirty-Four

Wyatt

I'm still piecing it together so that it's concise and coherent before I explain it all to my family. No, I didn't come to grips with the losses while I had weeks in my own head, but I had time to grieve. I feel more at peace. It was cleansing, to say the least.

The day was perfect. No, that's not right. It was beyond perfect. It was spectacular and wickedly unexpected. It felt like a dream with cherubs, pixies, dragons and crazy apple wielding wicked witches. We were happy. It was the first time in my life that I could say that the despair wasn't hanging around us, that the fog had lifted.

It's heartbreaking. Our family unit has gone from five to three in less than a year. None of that is even close to being the hardest part to handle. We'll still have to go over the will, and the company changes that will happen now whether I like it or not. Jamieson, Doll, and I will have to find a way to coexist in this new world.

While I was out of it, Whiskey didn't say much. Mainly, it was him just sitting in in the corner like a statue, reading his phone and texting away. Fuck, he looks just like Dad when he smiles. And Doll, I don't blame her for running fast. So now that Whiskey went out for burgers, I'm left in the silence of this barren room. Pressing the button for the nurse, she's here within minutes.

"Is everything all right Mr. Crown?"

"I'm totally fine. I just wondered if you could get me a computer, or a tablet so I can look up a few things."

"Of course. You had me worried. I'll see if someone has one you can borrow for a bit."

"Great. Thanks." I'm thinking of all that I want to find out about. How's the team doing? Who's in the lead? Is there info on our crash?

Coming back in, Sali holds a tablet in her hands with a massive smile. "The password for the Wi-Fi is already in, so you should be able to look up what you need." "Care for more Jell-O?"

I take the tablet in my right hand. "The green, please."

Chapter Thirty-Five

Wyatt

D

inner service." Swinging a Patties greasy paper bag in the air that smells heavenly, Dr. Callie enters my room about an hour later. "Your brother had to pop out. He asked Sali to get this to you, but she's with another patient." I open the bag and pull out the dangerous, yet delectable sweet potato curly fries, resting perfectly in a wax sack. The juicy burger smothered in chipotle mayo, with lettuce, a pickle spear skewered on top, and crumbled blue cheese pouring out the edges, is exactly what I needed. I feel my mouth water. Awesome.

"As your doctor, I'd suggest you not eat this at all. I feel it would demean the work we're doing to fix you." She smiles wide, steals one of the fries, then pushes the table over my bed, placing it all within reach.

"Pull up a seat, doctor. I'd like a bit of info if you wouldn't mind." She nods, grabs the metal rolling stool and sits beside me.

Yanking out the long, stringy, cardiac inducing goodness, I'm hungry as hell and happy to fill the void.

"How is she?" Dr. Callie forces a fake smile, popping a fry in her mouth.

"Sad, but she's doing good." Pulling out another fry, she eats it, resting back in the chair.

"Would she want to see me?" Grabbing up the burger in my opposite hand, pieces drip down. Taking a bite, I love the feel of it in my mouth. The juices, and the tangy sweet sauce couldn't taste any better.

"Mr. Crown, I gotta tell ya, she's been asking me about you every day. Well, until I shut her down. She wants to know how you are. She's wanted to know anything— something."

"Would you like me to arrange it. To see her, that is?" To see her. My skin itches and my heart pulls at the tethers holding it in place. It's not a want, it's a need.

"Yes, please."

"She's well enough. I think she'd be more than happy to make the trip here to see you, but I'd like you to get a bit more sleep first. How about tomorrow morning? We'll have her down here later in the morning?" Stealing another fry, she stands. "How about you get your fill and sleep a few hours. Tomorrow will come faster than you think."

Biting the burger, I lick my fingers free of sauce. Then, wiping my hand and the corners of my mouth, I mumble my thanks.

Chapter Thirty-Six

Circe

Yesterday was just another day at the park. Grueling physio regime, Mom visiting, Crane hitting on her mercilessly, eating all the crap food shoved at me, sucking back my pills, and sleeping. Yep. Fun, I tell ya.

Dr. Callie popped in a short while ago with news. Tomorrow morning, I'm going on a field trip. One of the Crown's wants to see me. Yes, I'm glad for the distraction, but I'm also scared. And glad. So glad. No, I'm ecstatic.

She told me to be ready at nine and not to look like I've have been for the past few weeks. She muttered something about how my appearance could earn me a recurring role as a zombie on The Walking Dead. Bitch. Yes, she's sweet, but honestly, she can pull a high grade 'dick move' better than most. So, with the assistance of my mom this morning, I showered, dressed nicer—no house coat or green unbuttoned hospital shift—combed out my hair and added a touch of makeup. It made me feel better, and closer to taking on the world than I have in weeks.

Looking at the clock, it's almost nine. Now, I'm scared.

"Mind if I help?" my mother asks.

"Thanks." Sitting in the wheelchair, waiting near the door for the doctor to return, my mother's smile is infectious. She knows I'm excited to find out the truth.

"You ready for today, Circe?"

Taking a deep breath, it catches in my chest, but it's better than it's been. The training has helped, and the opportunity to see Wyatt or Marca is pushing me forward gleefully. "More than I could ever imagine. I'm scared, hopeful, expectant, afraid, and seemingly happy."

"Do you want me there? I mean, I can just drop you at the door if you wish."

"Yes. Please, yes," I giggle. "Of course I want you there. If it's Wyatt, I want you to meet him. If it's Marca, then I need you there to help me deal."

Accepting my answer, she nods, smiles, and pushes the door open. Passing into the hall to await Dr. Callie, Sali meets us instead. "Ladies, good morning. This will be short. Both of you need rest."

"I get it. I'll be good, cross my fingers."

"It's supposed to be cross my heart. Crossing your fingers means you were promising to be bad," Sali quips off, laughing.

"Whatever works."

"All right, all right. Time to go," Dr. Callie joins us, a wide smile on her face.

Flanking my mother, the doctor and Sali lead us across the hall, then down the next hall across from the nurse's station. Stopping at the door directly in front of it, I realize this is where we saw China that day. We've been that close to each other? It makes sense they'd want to keep us close, but it was so close. I wish I'd known.

"Remember what I said, this will be short," Dr. Callie reiterates before entering the room.

"I'll be careful. Nothing too taxing. Got it."

Waiting by the door, the doctor and Sali enter first. Time passes slowly. It's like a movie in slow mo. I'm both anticipating and dreading it at the same time.

"We ready?"

Shaking my head, my mom pushes the cart through the doorway. Entering, I feel the tension of this meeting like a tangible enemy. The pressure in my chest increases, my heart beats out like a drum, and I'm sweating. I'm so afraid, it's not funny.

The room itself is sparse. I half-expected to find baskets of well-wishes and flowers abounding. There's nothing. Looking around the room, the curtain is drawn, and the window shade is drawn partway, holding the sunshine at bay. The machines are switched off, pushed to the side, away from whoever's in the bed. The doctor peeks her head in, speaks to the person, then slowly draws the curtain back. It's like a reveal on the dating game.

"Hello, Siren."

I'm speechless, stunned to silence. Testing every emotion, my body tightens. Everything I've wanted to know for weeks has come to fruition. I'm so afraid that it's an apparition, a ghost.

"Are you going to speak, love?"

Tears start down my face. I'm so happy, yet saddened. "Wyatt?" My voice cracks, failing me.

"Remember what I said you two. Gentle, easy, and short. Both of you back to your respected corners quick," Dr. Callie says.

Without an answer from either of us, my mother answers for me. "They'll be good."

"I'm going to leave you together for a bit, but if you need us, please hit the button. Either of you feel bad, you tell us right away," Sali states as she and the doctor leave. Both of them are smiling like Cheshire cats as they exit, while Wyatt, my mother, and myself are left alone.

Silence reigns supreme in the room as we both sit there, staring at each other.

"So, um, this is kind of awkward," my mother says, interrupting the pregnant air. "I'm Natalie, by the way."

Watching as Wyatt gives that beaming smile I love—that I missed—he reaches out his hand to take hers. It's weak and shaky, something I've never seen. Wyatt isn't weak or sapless. Wyatt is strong, resilient, powerful, and infallible.

"I'm Casper Crown. Or, to my Siren, I'm Wyatt. It's nice to meet you, Natalie." Even though he's talking to my mother, his full attention is still on me. Once the curtain was pulled back, we were hooked. Just like always, just the same. Nothing has changed.

He's everyone's Casper, and my Wyatt. The other half of me.

"I hear that you've been caring for my Siren. Thank you." His gaze is electric. I feel alight instantly, just like I always do.

I believe I always will.

"I'm not sure how much they told you, Casper, but I'm Natalie Matcheson. Circe is my daughter." Looking out the corner of my eye at my mother, she's anxious and panicked. Wyatt is calm and serene.

Even though I'm not secured to the chair, or held down, I'm afraid to move forward. None of it feels real yet.

"It's really you."

Wyatt understands. He understands my fear. "Yes, love, I'm here." His face changes from gleeful to sorrowful in the blink of an eye.

I lift up, just slightly, so that I can reach my hand out. I have to touch him and feel that he's tangible, real. But, my mother left my chair at the end of the bed where we first came in. It's not nearly close enough.

"Hold up there, young lady," my mother pipes up. Rushing around to my side of the bed, she pushes my chair closer to where Wyatt sits regally. I can finally touch him. My knees are tucked under the framework, and my chest is just inches away from the cushion, but it's close enough for now.

My heart is still. I don't feel it beat. I don't feel my breath as it rises and falls either. The pressure of being so close and not close enough is elusive. I want to be within his arms, held and secure. Bringing me closer, he smiles that glorious Crown smile that only Wyatt can. Only the happy and contented Wyatt can.

Checking him out, I see the damage that still riddles his body. His far hand is lying across the bed, wrapped and bandaged, and the close one, the one I want to have touch me, is tucked under the blanket. I'm still casted on the right at the wrist, but I need his touch so bad, I'll accept a twinge of pain. Pulling up my casted arm slowly, so as not to hit the bed, I lay it across his.

Wyatt pulls back the blanket with a wicked smirk. "It seems we have a matching set."

"Wyatt, I—" There's no way to stop the flow of tears as they stream down my face. Joy or sorrow, happiness or pain, I'm not sure which, but they're a dike I can't staunch.

"I missed you," Wyatt says. "I'm sorry you were kept away." Turning slightly on the bed, he leans toward me. Sadness pulls across his features as he explains further. "It was so dark. Being in my head was in a place I couldn't be with you, and it hurt. I could just imagine it for you."

"I—I was so alone." Choking out the words, my throat is tight, scratchy, and my heart constricts.

"You know, you kept me sane, Siren. You called to me."

"Will you tell me about it, please."

Closing his eyes, he leans back on the stacked pillows and breathes deeply. "Soon, Siren. Soon."

"I think you two have had enough for today," I hear my mother say. I'd forgotten we weren't alone.

Wyatt nods, then smiles and asks, "Will you stay while as I fall asleep?"

You'd think my heart just shattered. I know my soul fell to pieces as I fell more and more in love with him right then and there.

"I don't want to leave you at all. I've waited weeks to see you, and I can't think of leaving you. So yes." As the tears fall, I lay my head on the bed by his body, soaking up his warmth. I can't think of anything. I can't excuse myself from this, and I won't be moved until I have to. Even then, I'll be kicking and screaming. If I was in a body cast, I would find a way to be with him, touching him in some way.

Hoping that we've passed through the worst of it, that we can start to repair our bodies, minds, and souls, I relish the time I have with him.

It could have been minutes, hours, or the passing of a lifetime, but I was happy. I was at peace all within the confines of Wyatt's quiet room.

Listening to his strong heartbeat, I hear his breathing steadily slow as he falls asleep beside me.

This is where I belong.

Chapter Thirty-Seven

China

A

re you fucking kidding me! This is bullshit." I know it's unladylike, and my father would be rolling over in his grave for my conduct. But he's not here, so I don't give a shit.

We left my ride sitting on the curb, unprotected, available for every asshole to peel apart. I'm still pissed at that. How can the police officer have that much disrespect for fine machinery?

"Oh, honey. That one out there, he isn't one who falls for a pretty face who cusses at him. You need *sugar*, sugar." My roommate and cell aficionado has told me yet again how screaming at the police will get me nowhere.

Bullshit.

You just need the right equipment and flair, I believe. Correct me if I'm wrong, but a lady should wear something more modest. My cellmate's equipment is uncouth, with her—and I use *her* loosely—fishnets that are ripped in multiple areas, purple peeling and scuffed heels, and a skirt that should be a tube top. The nonexistent shirt, which is see-through, is a blush pink over a black lace bra. It's not necessarily going to gain her points toward me, let alone police officers. She explained herself as a purveyor of dreams, a professional supplier of happiness. She then said she was arrested for just looking stunning. It was a 'travesty' of justice, as she put it.

Fearing disease, I won't sit on any of the surfaces in the room. Most definitely, I won't take any advice from the defunct *purveyor of dreams* either. My lovely cellmate, Jucinda, even with her lack of clothing, is a very, *very* large woman. I'm tall, but she puts me to shame. With her six foot plus frame, linebacker shoulders, thin hips and twelve o'clock shadow that's just starting to peek out from under her meticulously caked on makeup, she's something. I'm progressive, and I can handle her, but I'd rather not cozy up to her today, not with the mood I'm in.

I'm pissy enough to spew something hurtful, and that would *not* do me justice.

My noble knight in shining armor and I arrived here a little over an hour ago. He had me processed, fingerprinted, photographed, strip searched by a not-so-lovely lady officer, and then plopped me unceremoniously in this filthy cell. Using my final and only call to Whiskey, leaving him a scathing message that will hopefully reach its destination, I awaited my ride. He needs to do everything he can to get my ass out of here, and *fast*. My charges are unpaid parking tickets, a summons to appear on excessive speeding (of which I'm very proud of). Ninety-two in a sixty, thank you very much. Then, another few racing charges, and a pussy taillight out with outdated insurance. If I keep up the noise, the arresting officer might come back so I can give him a bigger piece of my mind.

Jackass.

On the ride over, I laid into him about the whole scenario. The bullshit tickets, the unnecessary arrest, and of course the bracelets that were lovely, but not necessary. There's no way I was going to run off, and I absolutely hated sitting on my hands. He knew who I was, and I think it kind of scared him. He *had* to arrest me.

He spoke to someone a few times on his cell about having me in custody, and whoever it was, they were adamant about me being brought in, Judge's orders. Fuck me if I'm wrong, but he seemed to be warring with it personally. It seems our predicament was more about him. Either way, it meant shit. Still, the asshole brought me in for processing, put me in this newly appointed nine-by-nine space, and left me to my own devices.

As I wear a hole in the floor, pacing, the heavy metal door down the hall swings open. Scraping noisily across the floor, heavy footfalls smack on the cement as two distinct pairs of shoes clatter toward us.

"Time to go, princess." The first to enter is the evil jailer, Tiana. She joyously conducted my strip search. The second person stops a few feet away, and without looking, I know it's Whiskey.

Unlocking the door, Tiana motions for me to exit, then relocks the door behind me. I'd almost rather she put me back in after I get a look of my big brother's expression. I like the company of big Jucinda better.

"China," Whiskey barks.

"*Jamieson*. Nice of you to come." I'm more pissed at him than he could ever be of me, but I doubt it will get me far.

"Not another word, China May Crown. You hear me?" Whiskey growls. Nodding, checking my attitude, quietly I fall in step behind him and Tiana.

"Time to go." As Tiana motions, we follow, waving goodbye to Jucinda. Her jaw drops when she takes in the sight of Whiskey. Like all women do, she then lounges back on her bench and smiles sweetly.

After gathering my things, the keys to my bike—the bike that is no more—I follow Jamieson out of the station. I have the distinct feeling that my day isn't about to get any better.

Tiana tells me that I have to appear in court on the appointed day, and that if I don't, I'll have another bench warrant on my ass. Whiskey listens intently, taking in all the info necessary, accepting the paperwork before leading me to the door.

He's been deathly quiet. So quiet, I'm more afraid than ever.

A. He's never quiet. Not like this, at least.

B. Even though he's not a joker, he would normally quip a few snide remarks my way. He hasn't even talked to me.

I'm well and fucked.

Chapter Thirty-Eight

Wyatt

I woke up a little while ago, wondering where everyone was. Sitting in the coma, I heard, saw, and experienced the constant activity surrounding me. Now, there's no one *anywhere*. No Doll, no Whiskey, and no Siren.

Just before dozing off, I asked Natalie that Circe be brought back. Honestly, I don't have the heart to tell the story three times. I'll wait until we're all together. I kind of hoped that Doll and Whiskey would've been back already, but for some reason, they're not.

Taking this time alone, I feel out my body pains. Lifting each leg straight is straining and tiresome, but manageable. My chest hurts when I try to sit up, but I think that's just a side effect of being prone so long. The cast on my left arm is itchy as hell, and moving my fingers is difficult inside the plaster. They casted me from elbow to mid hand for stabilization, and it sucks.

My head is clearer than I think it's been in a long time. Hopefully, I won't have to rely on drugs. There's a high probability of it happening, but now I'll try to control myself better.

Then, there's my Siren. I want her to understand how much she's meant to me, and what it was that kept me sane inside that messed-up cerebellum of mine. Yeah, our relationship has been fast in terms of time together, but I've been in my head, thinking about her every second of the day. In the silence, all you do is think.

Pulling the side table back over, I grab a glass. Pouring myself some water, it mainly ends up all over the table. I've consumed at least two gallons of the fresh cool liquid, finding myself parched beyond measure. Dr. Callie said I might feel that way because of the drugs, and nurse Sali has been instrumental in refilling the jug. For all they've done, I'm immensely grateful, and Crown Industries will show that gratitude soon.

Hearing the door to the room open, I wait to see who's coming in.

"Hey," Doll says. It's not a happy 'hey.' That gives me concern. Both Doll and Whiskey walk through, scowling.

"What's going on?"

Looking at each other with glares and tight lips, they then focus their attention onto me with those same wide-eyed, *'he knows something'* stares. "Nothing," they say in unison.

Shaking my head, I turn to Whiskey, expecting a better response. He's tight-lipped and stoic, but whatever the two of them are hiding, I'm sure I'll find out soon enough. Nothing stays hidden for long.

"You look better, Cas. Do you need anything?" She hasn't called me Cas for weeks. I've listened. It's been Wyatt.

"I'm good, *China*. Actually, better than good." Pulling up the chair that had been pushed out of the way when Circe visited, Doll plops her long lithe frame into the seat, looking upset. "How was your ride?"

Her eyes bug out before she quickly schools her features. "Great. Uneventful, and somewhat relaxing."

"Glad to hear it. I was feeling bad you were stuck here." Pulling the cord that holds the button for the nurse and depressing it, I wait for Sali to arrive. Pushing up a bit taller in the bed, I power it into a sitting position.

"Yes, Mr. Crown," Sali greets.

"Could you please contact Natalie and Circe? If they're not too busy, I'd like to see if they're available to come back now."

"Yes, of course." Taking the uneaten tray with her, Sali leaves the room quickly.

"I could have called her or gone down. Sali didn't have to, Wyatt," Doll says softly. She's being sweet and nice, quiet and reserved. Nothing is more out of character for her. Something definitely happened today with these two clowns, and I'll get to the bottom of it quick enough. But it's not my priority. Telling them what happened that night is.

"Whiskey, can you grab a couple more chairs from the hall? We'll need them." He pockets his phone and nods. Once he's gone, I ask

Doll, "You're not getting out of telling me what's going on. Whatever it is between you two, I will find out." She purses her lips.

Nodding and leaving with a tight smile, she starts off. "I'll go help James."

There are times when our Crown stubborn streak is too much to take. I've learned over the course of this new predicament that life is too short, and not to sweat the little things. The one thing I do know is that I won't be left to figure this out alone. They'll be absorbed into the foray whether they like it or not.

Between my brother and sister, the two of them bring in three chairs. They're uncomfortable steel contraptions, but they'll do.

Holding the door open, poking around the opening with a grin, Sali enters. "Mr. Crown?"

"Please, call me Wyatt." Her eyes widen and she visibly looks flustered.

"I'm sorry." She weaves her hands in front of her, then finishes what she came to say. "Mrs. Matcheson and Ms. Maco will be down in a few minutes. Is there anything more I can get you? How is the pain?"

"I'm good, thanks. If you could give us about an hour of quiet without interruptions, that would be perfect." She nods, smiles, then leaves me with my mischievously sullen sister and brother.

I speak to both of them. "I want to make sure everyone is here. It's a story I don't want to go through more than once."

As the two of them settle into their chairs, there's a light knock on the door. "Hello?" Natalie says as she walks through. Backing Circe in slowly, Whiskey grabs the door.

"How is my Siren today?" I ask Natalie. I can't see Circe yet, but I'm expecting the smile to creep across my girl's face as I ask about her in the third person.

"You just had to pick up the phone and ask. I'm just down the hall. I'm sure if that was too much, you could have sent a carrier pigeon, or attempted Morse code." Sardonic wit. I missed that smart mouth of hers.

"Come over here, Siren."

Pushing her daughter close, tucking her in tight where she sat the other day, it's not close enough. I need her with me. Pushing up a bit, scooching across the mattress to the far side, I want her to join me on the tight bed. "Sit with me," I say.

Lifting from the chair with her good hand, Natalie assists her to the surface. Tucking in tight, I needed this like I need air in my lungs. As she settles under the covers, pushed right against my side, Circe lays her free hand under the cover. Touching my leg, it makes me want to be alone with her. It reminds me that so much has changed, in us. In me. In the family dynamics of the Crown's.

Because that's what this is.

This is *our* new family.

"I'm sure you've met China, my sister, and this is Jamieson, my brother. Natalie Matcheson is Circe's mother. Make her feel at home with us without fault. She's a part of this new family too." I kiss Circe on her forehead. "Our family has dwindled away. We need to care for it."

Looking around, everyone's quiet, soft and calm as they wait. I'm still not happy with this new burden, but I'll come to that later. For now, I have a lot to say, and no one but me can.

Thinking of what will start this right, an apology is what comes to mind. "I'm sorry." Turning toward my sister, she moves to say something, but I motion for her to wait. "I'm sorry for how much this will hurt to hear. Everything this year has made us stronger as it tore us down. But it also brought us together."

Thinking on that day, I take a deep breath. "Doll, you'd just gone out with the girls, and Whiskey wasn't expected to land until later. Mom was a flurry of emotions all morning, and I'd done my best to avoid her. All day, I did everything I could to stay far away. Around lunchtime, she'd called me over, asking me to join her in Dad's study. I was pissed off. The last place I felt she deserved to be was in there, but I knew if I didn't go, it could get bad. I was so mad. It felt like a violation of his memory to have her in there pulling it apart, ripping his soul to pieces. I was reluctant to, but I'm glad I did. She was on the floor, crying, pouring over pictures of *us*. There was a moment when I saw her for who she was; a woman grieving. She was lonely. She was lonely without him there, and she'd pushed us away so often that we didn't want to be near her."

Looking at each of them, Doll is tight and closed off with her arms crossed over her chest, holding herself together, but holding us at a distance. Whiskey is indifferent as usual. His eyes dart around the room, looking for an exit. He never felt her love any more than I did.

"We sat there on the floor for hours, laughing, flicking through pictures of Dad and us. It had been years since she'd gone in his room." Absently stroking the skin on Circe's arm, I think about it. I'm smiling, remembering what it was like when I saw her that day. I was ecstatic at how easily we got along. "She explained to me that she suffers from the same thing I do, manic moments that swing depressive.

"Dad was her fix. He was her drug of choice. When her episodes would take hold, he would pull her from her despair. His joy, and his infectious love would bring her happiness. She'd always hoped that us, her children, would be the joy that made her feel whole. And yes, we made her happy. We gave her joy in what we did, but it wasn't the same. She told me how sorry she was that she'd made us feel unwanted and unloved. She loved us, she just couldn't express it."

Rising from the chair, Whiskey paces the tight quarters. He hadn't been a part of this family for years. Dragging up the idea that she actually loved us might be too much for him to handle. Personally, I think he fights the same internal war we all fight. We deal with our own demons in different ways, only Jamieson ran to avoid the trigger of Marca Crown.

"Being trapped away in my head, I see it now. The way I was wasn't living. I was a ticking time bomb, just looking for the next best rush." Kissing Circe, showing her how much she means to me is a driving need. I can't get enough of her. I might be trading one high for another, but she's my personal heroine. Until I was locked away in my head, I hadn't noticed how much she'd meant.

"Doll?" She's trying to blend into the walls. "Did you know I heard you?" The confused look on her face tells me she doesn't understand. "Every day you sat here, bitched about how I needed to wake up, told me about your troubles, and nearly starved because of the food here. *I was here,* in my head, listening." Tapping the side of my head, I smile. "It was therapeutic hearing your voice." I look over at my sullen brother. "And Jamieson. I wanted to tell you what you wanted to hear. I heard your hurt and I need you to know, I'm here for you."

Stopping his pacing, Whiskey turns his chocolate eyes my way. Tears threaten his gaze. Nodding his head, the emotions he normally holds at bay surface, showing me how much he cares. In one sentence, he says it all. "Same. I'm always here for you, Wyatt."

Choking back the emotions, I continue with the story. "Mother wanted to come with me to get Circe at the airport. We'd already started talking, and I guess she just wanted to keep the dialogue going. So we took her car. Mine didn't leave enough room for luggage and an extra passenger. Things were good." I squeeze Circe's hand, knowing she's thinking on her panic attack. I know she's blaming herself for the predicament. "We talked more about what she planned for each of us, and I listened for once. Everything was fine at the airport. On the way home, from what I gather, a transport lost its wheel in the other lane. It jackknifed and careened into us, bouncing us a few times against the guardrail. We were flipped. Circe, had loosened her belt to grab Mother's phone that fell. I think that's what saved you."

Pausing for a moment, I remember what it was like, what *it* looked like. Turning, I talk directly to Circe. "I remember waking at one point while they were cutting me out. I couldn't find you, Circe. Panicking, I freaked out. I thought you were thrown free, but the first responders told me they'd already pulled you out."

I won't tell them what it looked like to see mother's eyes wide in death. The blood slowly dripping from her head onto the white roses, the moment you know you've seen someone depart. I won't leave them that reminder. I'll keep it to myself. "As we laid there, waiting to be pulled out, I could see her reflection in the rearview mirror. The cracked and split glass showed serenity." Shaking off the memory, I continue. "She was at peace. That's all I saw. I didn't see her hurt, I didn't see her pain. I didn't see anything but her heart at ease." I can't contain the tears any longer. "The day had given me something I hope we'll always treasure. She loved us. I know she wanted to give us a second chance at loving each other as a family should."

I've told them everything, all of it right to the end. I think Mom would be happy and content that her children were together. That in the end, *she* had brought us together. Now, it's up to us to keep that intact.

Turning to my sister, I see that Doll is shell-shocked. Her face is guarded, her posture is still, tight, and contained. She's expressionless. For once, I don't know what she's thinking, and I don't know exactly how to help. Tears stream down her face, and whether they're of happiness and peace, or despair and sadness, I'm okay with it mentally. Even if physically I'm a bit damaged, I know we'll make it through this together.

Whiskey has stopped his pacing. Standing still in the room, looking at me with an expression I can't read, a lone tear streaks down his cheek. As he brushes it away with the back of his hand, he looks away. Pulling his phone from his pocket, he turns to the door quickly. "I need to go out. I'll be back later to check on you, Cas."

I'll give him all the time he needs to deal with this. "You'll be back soon, yeah?"

"Yeah," he says, clearing his throat. Growing up, I always saw him like Dad in stature, but in his expressiveness and contained rage, it was Mother all along. Pulling open the door, he leaves.

Rising from the chair, gathering her thin coat and purse, Doll leaves without a word after Whiskey. I know they'll be okay, and I know we'll figure out how to deal with this, but it still hurts that they left.

Natalie is pulling Kleenex after Kleenex out of the box beside her, dabbing her face to staunch the flow. I have the feeling I'll love this woman just like I love her daughter.

I ask Circe, "Did I do right by them? Was it too much too soon? Too little? Should I have given them more time to deal with me awake before telling them?"

Stroking my face, she smiles up at me. It lights up my soul. My sleeping mind imagined this so often that it still doesn't feel real. Kissing just above my collarbone, Circe tells me just what I need to hear.

"You did it just right, Wyatt. They haven't had weeks to deal with it like we have. Give them time." Pulling her toward me, I kiss her on the mouth. It's a simple peck, but it's sweet and gentle.

Clearing her throat, Natalie rises out of the chair. "Speaking of time, I'll give you a bit of time to yourselves." She tucks Circe's wheelchair into the side of the bed. "When you need me, just hit the button." Leaving the room, closing the door with a resounding click, I find a small part in my heart for her.

"What a lovely woman," I tell her after her mother leaves us. Stroking the beautiful russet hair that has been monopolizing my dreams for weeks, Circe smiles.

"She is. I'm glad she searched me out. We needed it." Pulling her closer to me, I turn as much as I can to touch every inch of her body available to me. This is the first time we've had time to speak to each other without interruptions, or chaperones, and I need to just know she's real.

Thinking on the one thing that makes this feel real, I tell her what I've come to almost say as a mantra for us. "Where have you been?"

Smiling and turning slightly, she says, "I called out for you every day." She taps her head. "I was here, waiting."

Thank you for waiting seems appropriate, but so short of the emotion I wish to convey. "I know everything has been fast. Like, light speed fast, but I love you, Circe."

Chapter Thirty-Nine

Circe

S

o, give me details." Carli squeals as she runs into my tiny hospital room. Tossing her jacket on the vacant chair, pulling up a spot on the end of my bed, she grins from ear to ear. Now that Wyatt is up, here she is, happy and joyous, showing up out of the blue and making me ecstatically happy.

"Hi, Car. Glad to see you too, lover." Moving my legs up a bit, I tuck my blankets around me.

Her smile is infectious. Day after day, I left pleading messages, but she ignored me. Obviously, my best friend *can* hold off. Giving me a cold shoulder was something I never expected in a million years from her. She'd told me that I was cut off until the 'Crown' awoke, and fuck me, she held to her word. Quite the bitch move, but yes, I'm glad she's here, and thankful she's on my side. I'm happy to know she'll be my rock even when shit hits.

"Sooo...tell me."

"I thought you were back in Indy working?"

She waves off my question. "Like I'd leave you here to deal with this alone."

Yeah, okay. Ain't that what you've done for the past three weeks? "Come on. *Why* are you here, Carli? Did you get fired?"

"Fuck no. He couldn't piss standing up without me." Rising up off the bed, she paces slowly around the room, "No. I had a pressing family matter that had me in town." Her look is far away, making me wonder what's going on. She never talks about them, and I'd always assumed they were back in Japan, *not* California.

"So what—"

"Stop avoiding and tell me. How does the bike god look?"

Thinking hard and long on it, I say, "Serene." With a stargazing look—yeah, I know that's how I look because that's how I feel—I'm beaming with a sense of overwhelming joy.

"Serene?" Carli snaps. "Shit ain't serene? The boy is busted, was bleeding, lost family, not once, but twice, and you think he's serene?" Her face is somber and rightly so. She's right. "Watch that one. He's hiding and his crash is still inevitable."

I know she's right. I'm just afraid to face it. I'm deathly afraid that this ride isn't over.

Chapter Forty

Wyatt

It's quiet again.

Tired and worn out, Circe was taken back to her room. But neither my brother, nor my sister have come back. Once more, I'm alone with my thoughts.

Is it shit? You bet it is.

I'm relieved that I've told them about *that* day. How we were in the house, and on the ride over. But I'm keeping the memory of her and those final moments to myself. My sister is too soft to know the truth of how she died; how she looked as she died. I can't bring myself to go through that with her. Whiskey, on the other hand, *couldn't* care. Their relationship was the most volatile and convoluted of us all.

It's been a few hours since they left, and all of it cycles on reels in my head. Constricting me, it's tightening on my damaged soul like a vice. I won't bother Circe, and I don't know Natalie enough. I'm sure my friends are too busy to run here when I'm about to panic as well, so I do the only thing that I know is right.

As the room starts to squeeze me, pressing the button for the nurse, I wait for Sali to arrive.

Mere moments later, entering with a smile, it fades quickly as she sees the state I'm in. "Mr. Crown?" Her voice expresses how I *think* I look.

"I'm having a bit of trouble. Could you sit here and just talk for a moment or two?"

Her face shows her surprise, and I'm grateful for the elder nurse. Pulling on the chair beside the bed, she sits. "Sure. I can spare all the time you need. What would you like to talk about?"

"I'm not sure where to start." Telling her that is more truth than fiction. There's so much to our story that starting at one point will start another, and another, and another to complicate the first.

"Start where you need to, where you feel comfortable."

"I'm terrified." Saying it aloud makes it even more apparent. "I'm utterly and truly fucking terrified that I'll fail. That everything they expect...no, *demand* of me, will be in vain. You see, I always mess things up. This head of mine *always* messes it up." A lone tear falls down my cheek, tempting its brethren to follow. Wiping it away, I laugh at the silliness of it. "I'm sorry. I think being stuck in my head for so long has left everything close to the surface. Every emotion, every fear, every fucking—excuse my language—"

"No excuse necessary, Mr. Crown. Swear away."

"Everything is dangerous." Picking up the water, I sip it down through the flimsy blue straw, while Sali waits without saying a word. Placing it back on the table, I do my best to arrange my thoughts. "I'm not sure how much my sister or brother have told you about me."

"Not much, other than medical requirements."

"I deal with manic depression, and not well, I might add. Right now, I'm having a hard time coping."

"We can get you assessed."

"Assessed?" I say angrily. "I don't mean to be sharp, but assessment isn't what I need. I need something to lull this," I smack my head harshly, "back to sleep."

"Sleep isn't what you require. I doubt it would—"

"Sali, I'd hoped you were able to assist me, help me deal with these dangerous thoughts that run rampant. They're evil fucking nightmares of her death. The last goddamn moments of her in that car!" My jaw ticks as I feel every muscle in my body tightening to the point of crushing me once more. Sure, my mother isn't here, and she never will again, but even speaking of her boils it all down to the same keynotes in my concerto.

Rising from the chair, I see that Sali is reluctant to leave me. Warring with her decision, the fear to leave me alone is more pressing than to stay and see me fall apart. Coming toward me, she presses the button for the nurse's station.

"You were going to hang with me, listening, talking, not having me assessed, Sali!" I'd expected more from her. As the feeling crawls across my skin, I know what happens next. As the darkness absorbs all light in my soul, my mind scrambles. My pain increases exponentially, and every cell in my body feels sharper. I'm ready to take on any fight.

Other nurses walk in. They speak to Sali as I rant and rail about how assessment is definitely not what I need. "All I want is a way to forget! All I want is to forget it all. I need to escape the pain of seeing her final moments, the light leaving her eyes. Can't you understand how incredibly dangerous it is to see it? To feel it all?" The fire is banking the feelings to a boiling point. "Please, take it away? Please help me fight this?" I cry out as the pain surrounds me.

"It'll all be better in a moment..." Is the last thing I hear Sali say before I black out.

Chapter Forty-One

China

Hello?"

"We request you come back to the hospital, please. Wyatt's had an...episode," Sali informs me.

"Fuck! You've got to be kidding me?"

"No, I'm sorry. I'm not, China. You *really* need to come back. He'll need you."

"Did his heart fail again?"

In the background is loud shouting and noises. I can barely make out what Sali says. "No. He's *physically* well."

Shit. That's not good. "I'm just downstairs. I'll be right up," I say, ending the call. Making my way back to the building, I resign myself to the fact that this might not be something *I* can help with.

Rushing to the elevator, I'm thankful when it opens on the first push. Selecting the floor, watching it close up to slow for my liking, I take a moment alone to deal with this.

Watching the floors tick down, I mutter to myself. "Wyatt, what the hell am I going to do with you? What are you hiding?"

Fuck. When he was telling us about the crash I knew, I just fucking knew he was keeping something back. He didn't want to hurt me, so he's hurting himself instead.

Typical Wyatt.

As the door opens, I step into the hall, but instead of walking to his room, I turn left instead.

I burst through the door. "Circe, I need you *right now*."

The look on her face is one of true shock. Taking in what I'm saying, she's about to speak before another chimes in.

"Hi. Glad to meet you. Thanks for stopping by, but we were in the middle of a conversation." Sitting in the chair beside the bed, a tall Asian woman harnesses her inner bitch. At any other time, I think we could be *besties*, but at this moment, it's just annoying.

"I don't have time for this shit." Bringing the wheelchair over, I push it to the side of the bed. "Not to be rude—"

"Because you were," she interrupts again with a squinted look.

"Yeah. Look, I'm not worried about hurting your *last* feeling," I say, staring her down. "*But,* there's something important that requires your attention, Circe. Immediately." Without a question or a word, she begins lifting the blankets, dragging her tired body into the wheelchair.

"It's okay, Car. If China says I'm needed, I know she doesn't ask without really needing me."

At least *someone* here is listening. "Totally true. Now, let's get this show on the road."

"Excuse me, but no. China Crown ignored your ass for weeks *on end* in this place. She kept you from knowing—quite legally, I might add—and now I'm wondering why you're ready to bounce out of here when she snaps her manicured fingers. Please, tell me why, Circe?" The friend rises off the chair, pressing down her neat linen pants, standing to her full height. She's expecting to halt our departure. Good luck.

"Look. Pissing match aside, you're just gonna have to give me shit later. I *need* Circe."

Gingerly moving to the chair, she shifts her IV pole around. "Carli, it's fine. Yeah, I get all of those reasons, and they're totally valid points, but I need to go with China."

Thank you. Would I like to argue further and entertain myself with a battle of wills? Yeah, sure I would, but we need to go.

After Circe is settled, I start for the door without another word to the friend. Do I get her defense of Circe? Yep. My Harlow would have had anyone's ass in a sling for the move I pulled, but as it is, someone needs us more.

Stepping as fast as I can, I push Circe's chair out the door. "You're about to get the crash course in Casper Crown. I'm sorry, but there's no other way. I think that for once I'm just not enough."

"What's happening, China?"

"I can't even begin to explain it. You have to see it to believe what's going on with my brother. I'm hoping the connection you two have will be enough to settle him."

Chapter Forty-Two

Circe

Okay, I can do this. Wanting to be a part of Wyatt's life means I need to take the bad and good, right?

As China wheels me out of the room, the first thing I hear are the sounds of shouting, cursing, and Wyatt's voice breaking in pain. Why didn't I hear it before? Have I been that involved in myself that I didn't notice things going on? Fuck.

Trying to ignore my oversight, placing all of my concentration on the one pushing my stroller, I admonish my selfishness.

"I'm putting faith in you, Circe. I hope you can do what I've done, but better." Every ounce of what China says strikes a chord. "Honestly, I've seen you two together, and I'm sorry I kept you away. And yeah, I suck at apologies, but if you can help, I promise not to leave you in the dark again."

"You're right. You suck at apologies. But it's not about me or you. This is for Wyatt, yeah?"

"Damn straight. But it won't be pretty." Pushing the door to his room with her ass open, the crashing sound of Wyatt increases.

"I don't need that!" Slamming his casted arm into the side table, the sound echoes off the walls, the smashing plaster flying everywhere.

"Circe," China warns. "If you want, I can wheel you out. Don't be afraid to say this is too much."

"China, move me, please."

"Out or in?"

"In."

Avoiding the extra nurses, security, and Dr. Callie, China pulls my chair up to the end of the bed where there's the least traffic. Taking in all of Wyatt, his eyes are vacant. He's far off in his own turbulent storm, fighting a battle of wills. Pain and control are not mutually exclusive, and he's not winning.

"Wyatt," I say softly at first, then more forceful a second time when he doesn't acknowledge me. "Wyatt!"

Over the din of confusion and hospital care workers, no one hears me. Looking behind me, up to China, I see the fright. She's about to fall apart and no one see's how painful this is for her too. Watching as they try to restrain and contain him, I feel horrible for both of them if this is the way it's always been.

Is this how everyone has thought to care for his issue? Further containment and less understanding? Well, not me.

"Circe. You shouldn't be here right now. It's not safe," the doctor states, trying to feed a full syringe of opiates into the IV line.

"Dr. Callie. Could you leave us alone?"

"Just let me get this—"

"No. I mean, before you drug him," I state emphatically.

"Circe, I don't think you understand. He's harming himself. We need to control—"

"That's the problem, doctor. I think all anyone has ever done is control him. Please, let me try it another way."

Turning to Wyatt's sister, Dr. Callie thinks she'll find a defender. "China, I—"

"I agree with Circe. Please, everyone leave. And I don't mean *after* you dope him up." Watching her request be ignored, they still work away, attaching cuffs. Her patience wanes. "Now!" she hollers.

As they pause, releasing Wyatt's hand, he calms. "Everyone, please leave," I tell them, as China ventures to the door, opening it wide.

"All of you leave, please." The harsh face of determination, a perfected resting bitch face, China smacks the door lightly to grab their attention. "Let's go. We've got this. And if by chance we don't, you can come back and tell us we told you so."

Walking away, one by one, each look at us with incredulity. They're amazed we *want* to deal with this alone.

Looking back over her shoulder as she's leaving, Dr. Callie places the cap back on the tiny syringe. Turning to China with a crestfallen expression, she says, "We'll just be outside the door."

We understand what we're asking, and we're ready to accept it.

Turning my attention back to Wyatt, I see the physical stress of everything as his body tenses. His eyes dart and the darkness fills him. No, I've never dealt with anything like this, but I feel the same despair anytime I think back to my crash. Anytime I have a panic attack, my soul crushes just a tiny bit. When I see him being dragged under like this, I don't *just* understand it, I appreciate the coping mechanisms he's devised.

As the door shuts and the room quiets, I ask for help. "China. Could you wheel me up to the side?"

"Yeah, sure. One sec." Bringing me to the edge where I sat only a day ago, China clicks the lock on the wheels. "I'm sorry you're seeing the worst of it."

"I'm not seeing the worst of anything, Doll." I lift myself slightly out of the chair. "You can go. Don't worry, I have this."

"Circe, it's one thing to get a crash course, but it's another to hop into the lion's den without a stick to beat it back with."

"He won't hurt me. It's okay." Placing my hand on the bed, I move toward the empty space beside Wyatt. "Really, I'm fine. We'll be fine."

I push up higher until I can lift myself to sit on the edge. Stroking Wyatt's sweat-soaked platinum hair, I reel at the pain he's in.

"If you need me, I'm right outside."

Hearing her leave me, I take in all of Wyatt. His cast is destroyed, which will cause him delays in riding. His wild eyes dance untrained on nothing specific. His hospital gown and hair are soaked with sweat. Leaning into the hard bed, turning my attention elsewhere, I don't notice if China left or not. It doesn't matter. All that matters is him and his pain.

"Wyatt?" Touching his hair, I stroke the side of his strong jaw as it ticks, trying to calm him. No, I won't be a fix, but maybe I can be a relief. "Wyatt, I'm here. It's Circe."

Since the doctors and nurses left, he's calmed considerably. The stress of them in no way made it better, it just cornered the beast. Now the fight or flight has lessened, but the beast is still wary.

"Do you remember the first time we kissed? I thought you were a pompous man, only looking for your next thrill, your next fuck. The next war. You know what I saw, though, and I never voiced it? I saw you hiding. That guy on the track, he'd hurt you more than if you'd hit him, didn't he? The fear of causing someone else's pain scared you. You were afraid that *you* could have been the catalyst for another sad family." Keeping my voice calm and serene, I tuck in tighter to Wyatt's side, laying my casted arm across his body.

"I know what you saw that day. You held back from telling them. I get it. You didn't want to tell your brother or sister what you saw in the car when we crashed, did you?"

Moving his hand, he finally touches me. He's relaxing.

"You saw it too?" he asks.

Answering his question, tears choke my voice. "I saw death." I know he was there. I knew he took a life, and I knew it was going to be painful. With tears threatening my eyes, I take in a deep breath. "There was nothing you could do."

He doesn't reply right away. Instead, he stays quiet, in his own system of containment. "The part that pains me most is that I was glad for her. She needed the peace. That, and I don't think I could've survived you gone from my life. You understand that, right? Without you, with me—in here—you saved me every day." Tapping his head, he finally turns his eyes from the ceiling to look at me. As the wetness coats his cheeks from tears, I see it all. Pain and suffering, joy and relief.

It's true, we haven't known each other long, but I have a connection to him that I can't deny. Seeing the change in him, I feel that his turbulent ocean has lulled. It's not gone, it's just relinquishing its hold slightly, allowing him control behind the wheel.

Thumbing his tears, I listen as he talks. "You were what I thought of. You were all that kept me going as I sat here, wondering about everything. It was all wrapped up in you. I'm not sure if I'm moving a dependency from racing and sex to you, but I *know* I can't do this alone, Circe. Please, tell me this isn't a dream?"

"I'm here, Wyatt, and we'll figure it out." Kissing his cheek, I taste the salt of his tears. Turning his head slightly, he kisses me and I feel every ounce of passion in his lips. My heart skips a few beats, and my soul cheers for more. Breaking away, I tell him again. "I'm here. I'm not leaving."

Pulling back, he stares into my eyes. "Thank you for calling me, Siren."

I smile. "I'm glad you answered."

Prologue

Wyatt
Three Months Later

Days have passed. I've been learning to grab things, pulling and pushing, along with other stupid stuff to gain control of my body. Shit like flexing your fingers is crap if you ask me, but I can write my name again. I can stand without feeling queasy now, and hopefully, I'll be able hold a throttle. But I'll never race again.

All day, every day, it's been me and Circe as we've tried to repair all the broken pieces of our badly damaged bodies. When I say Circe and I, I mean it in the terms that she's been what's cooled me. She's calmed me and made me feel whole when all I wanted was to collapse in my mind. Finding a way to settle my mind without the rush of a track and without sex has been hard. I sat confined in my head and despised returning to a dependency on drugs. I'd thought I'd found peace in that coma, but that was a lie.

It's been two weeks since the last episode. I should have been put into a mental institute for the way I behaved, but Circe stayed.

That sneaky sister of mine, she saw it. She understood it far better than I gave her credit for. Yeah, she'd always been my rock in the situations with Mother, but thrusting myself into despair, feeling that I was unfairly blaming our mother for everything... well, let's just say it all came crashing down. If she hadn't brought Circe to me, and reminded me of what I was caring for, I'm not sure I could have stayed out of that rubber room.

I'll forever be grateful that she knew what I needed. It was *her*, my Siren calling me, dragging me back, helping me see the light at the end of my dark tunnel.

The first time she'd really had a clear picture of what an episode of mine is like was when I was smashing things. Losing my calm exterior and invariably destroying everything around me and within, she saw it all. Without her pushing me to it, it wouldn't have been possible to get me to listen. I needed the help of the hospital psychologists to combat my mania, and she knew it.

I'd always dealt with the resulting pressure of never being enough when it came to my mother's attention. I'd felt it was my fault for not being a better person, or a better son to her. After the day of clarity we had before the accident, I realized it wasn't just me that suffered. We all did. And no, I don't just mean me and her, I mean it as in all of us. Wyatt the son had found his place in her heart for a day, but it took an accident for me to find a stable position where I didn't blame *us* anymore. It wasn't our fault.

It took a while for Whiskey and Doll to come to grips with the final moments of our mother's passing too. The shrink had us all together so that we could hash it out. They'd never had the chance to see the peace, the utter and complete calm that settled over her. And because they'd missed it, they'd only ever had the reception of cold, calloused and harsh Marca Crown. I felt for a while that they'd been robbed of it, that at some point, it was my problem and my fault. Circe straightened my ass out about that pretty damn quick, as did the Dr. Marshall.

No, I'm still not settled with her death. No, I definitely don't feel settled with our parents' decision to leave me in charge of everything. And most emphatically, I don't feel that they gave my brother the position he was born for. He's a truer leader than I. But the past is past, and that was their call. We have to abide by it, for now.

It's funny. Things are almost normal now. A little over a week ago, Circe moved into my room. Her chest took a bit more time to recover from than they'd hoped, and my head was constantly monitored, if not regulated.

Doll and Whiskey are still hiding something from me, but I'll get to the bottom of it eventually. They have quiet conversations that die down when I'm close, and it's pissing me off. It hurts to think they don't want to let me in on whatever it is, but they'll come around.

Doll, of course, is back to her usual antics in the public eye. She's racing and off doing what Doll does. We celebrated her birthday in the hospital before Whiskey flew out again last week, and I was saddened to see him go. The will wasn't holding him here, and I think Mom and Dad knew it wouldn't. He needs the snow like we need burnt rubber.

We've never really had a chance to be brothers, and now that our family is smaller, I'm a bit desperate to fix that. We'll never be close, as too much has separated us. It's not age, but decisions that have directed us apart.

After Mother's burial, the police brought me her effects from the accident. It hurt at first to see the carnage. The worst of it was her phone. She had snapshots in there of each of us that were candid. I was barreling around the track in one, sitting on the back porch in folded down race gear, talking to Dad. His hands are pointed out to a spot on the track with a larger than life smile, and I'm caught mid-laugh with my face lit up. There were ones of Doll in the kitchen, pouring over her cereal while reading a bike magazine. There's one out on the track with her hair whipping behind her at breakneck speeds, and even sneaky shots through the door as she did her makeup.

Surprisingly, there were pictures of Jamieson. She'd snuck out to his trials, his competitions, his training days, and none of us knew she'd done it. I think it made it more heartbreaking that we always felt she was callous and heartless toward us. She was more loving than we knew. She just didn't know how to show us.

It's amazing the things you see when the mirror is cracked. We'd always seen her as the heartless person who couldn't give us the time of day. We were wrong—so wrong. Every day, I thank the heavens that I had that moment. Heartbreaking, yes, but it's something I'll treasure forever.

"Hello?" After a light knock on the door, Sali pops her head into the room. Circe is down at the café with her mother, enjoying a coffee, and I was just trying to shave with my opposite hand.

“Hello,” I greet her from the washroom, shaving cream covering half my face. There are bits of toilet paper sticking here and there from my mishaps. Stepping out of the small alcove, Sali is more than grinning, she’s beaming.

“Mr. Crown, I was asked by an ambulance attendant to give this to you. They’d found it at the scene, and had forgotten all about it until they were cleaning out their locker at the hall. You were gripping it tightly, he said.” She hands me a small black felt bag with a tiny box inside, the tiny box I thought I’d lost.

“I wondered where that went. Thank you.” She nods her head, then starts back toward the door.

“By the way. She’s the one, Wyatt,” Sali states with a nod, smirking like a Cheshire cat. It’s the first and only time she calls me by my name, and she’s one hundred percent right.

“Yes. Yes, she is.”

Extras

Want more? Check out the first chapter of *Risen*, The Crashed Series Book Three.

Prologue

Jamieson

The Past

The biting winds as trees whip past at breakneck speeds, cutting the snow's harsh edges with my board is the best feeling. Well, besides this.

"Yes! Yes! Yes!" she screams as I pound into her, all while smacking her ass. I love the look of the red welts that rise. Pushing her body into the wall, flattening her chest against it, my hips piston faster and faster knowing my end is near.

"More, Whiskey, more! Please!" she pants, smiling through the abuse.

"Hold on." I spread her legs wider and grip her hips tight. The woman in front of me is taking everything I'm giving her. Her squeals, screams, and moans push me toward my end with a fervor.

Slapping her ass cheek again, I watch as the red lines rise. Knowing I'm seconds from release, my body takes over and my mind clears of all thoughts but this moment. *In and out. In and out.* The animalistic need controls me. With a few final thrusts, my body shakes and shivers. Grinding out, growling my end, my need is slaked.

For the moment.

Grunting as I pull back from her body, holding the condom in place, she whines when the fullness ends. "Whiskey."

Moving away toward the trash, I wrap up the package and toss it away before wandering off to start the shower, leaving her standing in my bedroom.

With the water rushing out, I don't hear her come up behind me. Wrapping her arms around my body, she kisses my back. I'm ignoring her because when I'm done, that's it. I always ignore them. They don't matter.

"Hey Whiskey, what do ya say we hit the far trail after? There's an abandoned cabin up there, and we could—"

"Sorry," I say as I open the shower door, "I have other plans today."

"Well, what about tomorrow? I could—"

Walking into the shower, I turn back to face her. "Look, it was fun..." I pause because I can't remember her name. "It was fun, but it's done."

"Jessica. My name is Jessica." She's pissy that I just fucked her against my wall after meeting her only a few hours ago. Hell, what did she expect?

"You walked up to me at the lift and asked for a ride. What made you think I cared what your name was?"

"Whiskey, I thought we had fun?"

"Yeah, we did, and it's done."

All women are needy and greedy. "I don't do relationships, and you'll never find me hanging around for breakfast, lunch, or dinner. I don't date." I close the door to the shower. "But thanks for the fun."

I don't turn to look to see if she's still there. I don't worry that she'll take something before she leaves as a souvenir, and I don't doubt that she'll throw something because they all do it. I'm so used to it now, I don't even balk at the damage.

When I'm done cleaning up, I exit the shower with only a towel and a smile. Walking into my spare bedroom, I find my Aunt Janie, smiling. It's a fake, but it's a smile, nonetheless.

"Another one bites the dust?"

Shrugging my shoulders, I head out of the room and dress. My room is down the hall, but I don't bring girls to my suite. It's my refuge. This is where they all get a piece of me, and I keep them separate from where I find peace.

"You know at some point, something is going to happen to you. The great Jamieson Crown will bow at the feet of a woman that will crush his ass. Your head will spin so fast, no amount of pussy will keep you entertained. She's going to cause you grief, and I'll stand back here, smiling and watching it all unfold with a shit-eating grin on my face."

My aunt is totally wrong. Nobody cares for me but me. No one will ever get past this cold heart again, and no one will ever shatter my soul. Been there, done that. It ain't happening again.

I go with bypassing the conversation we have every time one of these girls leave. "What's on the docket today?"

I don't worry about dressing around my aunt. She's seen me naked more than dressed. Pulling on a pair of tracks, leaving them low, I toss on a T-shirt.

"You have training with the Olympic team tomorrow, but there's nothing today. Why don't you hit the hills for a while? I can call in the chopper. Just have some *you* time, Jamieson."

"Yeah, I might do that." It's always *me* time. I'm always alone, and I like it that way.

"Did you see that Doll won another race yesterday?"

My little sister is taking the motorcycle world by storm, just like my little brother. The two of them are devils on two wheels, just like I'm a devil on a board. Give me snowcapped mountains and I'm satisfied. And that's why I'm alone. I need the cold, they need the heat.

"Yeah. I saw Dad won another one, too."

"You know, you should go visit soon. Isn't Wyatt's nineteenth birthday coming up?"

Shit. I should send him a card, or a stripper gram. That would piss of Mother. "Yeah. I'll give him a call later."

"You have a break in a few weeks, so why not go visit? Give him a present in person." She's always trying to repair the rift, but nothing ever will. We're just too different, and the past has ruined us all.

"Call the chopper, I'll head out in a few."

Knowing I've just shut down on her, Aunt Janie purses her lips and walks away. I don't even have to look because that's what she always does.

I wish I wasn't alone. I wish I had my family, but it was torn apart long ago, and I'm not the one to fix it.

About the Author

Mother of two insanely (well trained) sarcastic men, wife to a dangerously smolder inducing grumble bunny (my fireman), and one of the Three Biotches Professional Margarita Drinking team. Living in Northern Ontario (that place with white stuff), in Canada, by day I can be found biking the trails, snowboarding the hills or paddling on the lake. I work (dayslavery) to annoy customers and coworkers alike, putting a smile or an annoyed sneer on the face of all that I cross. I make sure that my husband has reasons to grow further grey hairs, many more wrinkles, and an opportunity to find the last drop in the bottom of many a drink. I can't turn down Marvel movies, I love drag racing, loud fueled cars, Starbucks coffee is my nemesis and without it I'd be a raging jerk all day, Football (the UK kind), motocross, knitting — non-professional sport of course — and I can get a mean swing-on in a hammock with a Margarita in hand.

Like you, my love of reading came from one simple book. Do I remember what it was, no, but it started me on a path that I'm so glad I've travelled. Every day I find new reasons to write twisted, mind warped stories that take you on fantastical rides. The men and women that grace the pages are possibly someone I've seen in real life at a ballgame, on a subway or merely in the coffee line. Be careful because your antics can become something I write about.

I'll say that it took a few years to find my groove, but I know now that torturing my characters is some of the greatest joys I've had in years. Love and loss can be equally heart wrenching and my stories reflect that. In the pages you can hope for the good guy to win, but it won't always happen and I won't promise that, because life doesn't always have a guaranteed HEA (happily ever after) or HFN (happy for now). Not all love is clean, there is darkness, there is hope, and those little moments where we find our HFN or HEA is where the light skips across our heart to make it beat just that tiny bit faster.

So as you flip the pages in my books, enjoy the OMG's and tears as you tear your hair out, toss a book or two, because I want you to feel their pain as if it were your own. As they live it, absorb it on the pages. Thank you for reading, thanks for being a friend, and I look forward to meeting you in the future for drinks, danger and laughs.

Visit Kerri at www.AuthorKerriAnn.com

Also by the Author

The Crash Series

Casper

Siren

Whiskey

Risen

The Broken Bows MC Series

Rook

King

Pawn

Gambit

The SoCal Soulless MC Series

Queen

Knight

Bishop's Play

The Hades Army MC Series

Death's Deal (Coming Soon)

Loyalty or Royalty (Coming Soon)

Standalone Novels

Bound by Fate

Last Breath

Charged

Rushed

Tied

If, Love

About the Publisher

Kingston Publishing Company, founded by C.K. Green is dedicated to providing authors an affordable way to turn their dream into a reality. We publish over 100+ titles annually in multiple formats including print and ebook across all major platforms.

We offer every service you will ever need to take an idea and publish a story. We are here to help authors make it in the industry. We want to provide a positive experience that will keep you coming back to us. Whether you want a traditional publisher who offers all the amenities a publishing company should or an author who prefers to self-publish, but needs additional help – we are here for you.

Now Accepting Manuscripts!

Please send query letter and manuscript to:

submissions@kingstonpublishing.com

Visit our website at www.kingstonpublishing.com[1]

1. https://kingstonpublishing-my.sharepoint.com/personal/crystal_kingstonpublishing_onmicrosoft_com/Documents/Clients/Lisa%20Colodny/Promises%20of%20Wishing%20Rock/www.kingstonpublishing.com

About the Publisher

Don't miss out!

Visit the website below and you can sign up to receive emails whenever Kerri Ann publishes a new book. There's no charge and no obligation.

https://books2read.com/r/B-A-SLJG-JXGU

BOOKS 2 READ

Connecting independent readers to independent writers.

Did you love *Siren*? Then you should read *Last Breath*[2] by Kerri Ann!

[3]

The lovers, the killers…The infamous.

Would I succumb or flourish? Would I be their next victim or the Bonnie to their Clydes?

My every fear pounded out to the sound of my heartbeat, telling me to run when they arrived covered in blood on my doorstep, but for the life of me I could not. I was drawn to their darkness and drowning in the need to feel what they feel. Their passion a welcome surprise.

Before their arrival on my doorstep, sadness pain and solitude were all that I had endured. I'd hoped for an escape from my small town where I'd been the addicts abandoned daughter, and the slave to a vile rage fuelled grandmother, but it never came. Until them. Salem and

---

2. https://books2read.com/u/4AYAae

3. https://books2read.com/u/4AYAae

Malachi, they were the breath of freedom needed offering a reprieve that could not be denied.

Salem's sweet grin, his mesmerizing, alluring soft eyes drew you in. His sensual touch that offered the boy next door, hid the psychotic soul seeping darkness that clouded any joy. The devil created Salem as his perfect muse for destruction. His angelic beauty was merely a facade for his sinister soul. Unless Malachi was by his side to balance his internal warring.

Malachi needed Salem as much as he needed blood in his veins. The visibly broken man with a damaged smile drew me in, calling me to follow him anywhere. I knew there was a softness to him and that he was a soul not unlike mine. Badly damaged but in need of love that would balance him.

My soul craved the world they offered and their mayhem was a dream I'd gladly chase regardless of consequence. Or so I thought.

It could mean my death.

Read more at https://www.authorkerriann.com.

www.ingramcontent.com/pod-product-compliance
Lightning Source LLC
LaVergne TN
LVHW010546160826
845677LV00013B/3018
* 9 7 9 8 2 2 4 4 9 6 5 0 1 *